Michelle Kwan

THE WINNING ATTITUDE!

WHAT IT TAKES TO BE A CHAMPION

AS TOLD TO LAURA JAMES

HYPERION BOOKS FOR CHILDREN
New York

Printed in United States of America

First Edition

10 9 8 7 6 5 4 3 2 1

The text for this book is set in Goudy 13/17.25

ISBN 0-7868-0546-3

To my parents, my grandparents, my brother Ron, my sister Karen, and to my extended skating family, who have all helped me to develop and maintain my winning attitude. —M.K.

TABLE OF CONTENTS

INTRODUCTION

The Thread of Gold

When I was five years old, my sister Karen and I started taking skating lessons at a little rink in southern California. We were just a couple of pipsqueaks, excited to be trying something new. We loved zooming around on the slippery ice and feeling the wind in our faces. Even falling made us laugh.

We started because we thought it would be fun. We were just following our hearts. When you're that little, that's all you should do. We were lucky because our parents hoped for nothing more for us than happiness. They had no way of knowing that sooner or later, childlike fun would lead us to bigger dreams and greater challenges. And they certainly had no way of knowing how soon this would happen for me.

When I was seven, I saw the 1988 Olympics on

TV. Suddenly my eyes were opened to truly great figure skating. Seeing the performances of people who stood at the very top of the skating world—people like Brian Boitano and Katarina Witt—revealed something to me that I hadn't realized till then. Somehow, in the middle of all that fun, skating had touched my heart. Amazingly enough, I've made it to the top with my idols. Of course, it's taken a lot more than just fun to get here. I've learned it takes a lot of dedication and hard work. But to this day, when I take that first step onto the ice in the morning, I'm still so excited that I have to catch my breath.

In this book, I want to tell you about the qualities that took me from that wide-eyed seven-year-old to where I am now. I want to show you the tools I needed to succeed, and give you my inside tips on how you can use the same techniques in your life. I want to share with you how you can make your own dreams come true.

Most of all, I hope reading this book will give you the best chance to succeed in whatever you set out to do. It might be something big, like becoming an actor or a dancer or a doctor. It might be something you've never done, like playing a musical instrument or programming a computer. You might want to excel at a sport such as soccer or basketball.

You might want to get straight A's in school. Or maybe you're just trying to get through a really tough book for English, like *Great Expectations* by Charles Dickens. This book is for all of you. You don't have to win an Olympic medal to be a champion. More than any medals, my skating itself is my proudest achievement.

When I set out on my journey, I felt like I had a huge mountain to climb. As I started up that mountain, I learned all kinds of unexpected things about myself. I saw my life, my goals, and my self in a whole new light.

Now I live in Lake Arrowhead, California, way up on a beautiful mountain, 5,500 feet above sea level. I train at a place called Ice Castle, one of the top facilities in the world. It's only a couple of minutes from my house, so I'm there all the time. They have to drag me off the ice at the end of my practice time. I say, "Let me just squeeze in one more jump!" "No, Michelle!" they say. "You're done. Come back later."

My love for skating hasn't stopped since I've reached the top. With every accomplishment, my love has grown. Even the disappointments I've had have made me love that slippery ice and the feeling of the wind in my face.

I stepped up to the top level in 1996 when I was fifteen years old, the year I won my first National and World Championships. Since then, I've won a lot of competitions. But there have also been a few big ones where I didn't win. If you've followed my career the last few years, you've seen me cry all kinds of tears. Tears of joy, of disappointment . . . I couldn't hide my feelings if I tried.

When you get to the top, your goals get extremely high, and the whole world seems to be holding its breath for you. With those kinds of expectations, even something great like a silver medal can feel, for a minute or two, like a failure.

I'll tell you honestly that getting the Olympic silver in Nagano in 1998 was one of the hardest moments of my life. I didn't know how I'd get over it, at first. The Olympic gold had been my dream for as long as I could remember.

At moments like that, the only thing that can save you is honesty. Honesty can hurt sometimes, so it helps when it comes from someone you love. Luckily I'm surrounded by people I trust—my family and my coach, Frank Carroll—who understand me and can help me through the most difficult times.

After the medals were handed out at Nagano, I asked Frank, "Why did it happen?" He looked me in the eye and told me honestly, "You held yourself back, Michelle. You didn't let go."

When the sting of honesty passes (it always does), what you're left with is truth.

As soon as I was able to accept that my best that night hadn't been good enough, I looked at my silver medal in a new light. I felt like that seven-year-old kid again. I thought, Look at me. I'm living my dream. I live and breathe and love skating with every ounce of my body. It's just how I imagined it would be back when I was a pipsqueak sitting in front of the TV with my mouth wide open.

Sometimes you just have to stop and appreciate your own accomplishments. I've had setbacks—everybody does—but they haven't managed to discourage me. If anything, they made me more determined to keep improving at the thing I love to do. Right after Nagano, I went to the World Championships in Minneapolis and came home with the gold.

I'm going to be honest with you in this book, like my friends and family are with me. If you want to know how to win first place every time you do something, then you've come to the wrong person. Anyone who tells you they can give you that secret is lying.

To me, winning means something more than finishing first. If you stick with something you love for a long time and give it your very best, then you're a winner—no matter how far you go, how you place, or if you place at all.

The love I have for skating runs through my whole life, like a golden thread. I can follow it all the way back to that first lesson and the fun Karen and I had slipping and sliding on the ice. Still having my passion for skating is my real reward. It can be yours, too, if you follow your heart and try always to be honest with yourself.

The 2002 Olympics in Salt Lake City aren't that far away. I still dream of that gold medal, and when I think of going there, I still have to catch my breath. But the medal is just one detail in my bigger dream of being the best skater I can be.

To get to the top of the skating world, I've relied a lot on my family to be honest with me. But I've also had to try to understand myself, honestly. Inside me there are certain qualities that have helped me do this. Some of them came naturally to me. Some I had to work at. Others were pulled out of me by my skating.

I've written down a list of these qualities, and they make up the first ten chapters of this book. These basic qualities are in everyone. You just have to find them, which is not always easy. There are questions and tips at the end of each chapter to help you find them in yourself.

The ten qualities I've focused on in Part I are all related to each other, like a family. One's no good without the other. Some resemble each other. Some have good twins and evil twins, some have cousins. You'll need to get to know them all.

The very first step is to find the thing you love—the beginning of that golden thread—and follow it. Then find where these qualities are hiding in you and let them help you turn your love into a passion. If you can find that passion, then you'll have the winning attitude. Even if only one other person knows you've found it—even if it's just you! — then you're a winner.

At a certain point, you may want to get more serious about your passion. That's what the second part of the book is about. Whether you want to be a more understanding sister or brother or you want to be a professional dancer, it takes a lot of commitment and sacrifice. So you'd better be prepared to be *really* honest now. In each chapter of Part II, I've posed some big questions to help you stay on track at whatever you're attempting.

No matter how far you go with your dream, never forget to enjoy what you do. Have fun. Try to laugh when you win and laugh when you fall. Okay, so maybe you'll cry when you fall, too. Either way, keep going. Falling's part of the game. It's like my dad always says: "No matter how good you are, the ice is still slippery." The important thing is, it's *your* ice.

PART I

Winning Qualities

CHAPTER ONE

Vision

SEEING SPARKS

I was just five years old when Karen and I started to skate. I thought skating was incredibly fun, but I didn't think too much about it. I didn't know anything about the Olympics or the long tradition of skating in America. I just felt comfortable at the rink. I loved charging across the ice and spinning around. Every week, I looked forward to my lessons. It was simple.

Then, when I was seven, I saw Brian Boitano skate for his gold medal at the 1988 Olympics. It was like a thunderbolt struck. Something sparked inside me, and when I saw him standing on the podium, that spark burst into flame.

Actually, I saw two things that night. One was outside me, and one was inside me. I could see that Brian put his whole heart and body into his skating.

My heart beat faster, and I knew right away that *that* was the way I wanted to skate. At exactly the same time, I saw the thing inside me: my dream was born.

It might sound like my dream was just the fantasy of a seven-year-old. All of us imagine ourselves doing fantastic things. We play at being movie stars, scientists, world-famous ballet dancers. Play and fantasy are great, because they help you grow your imagination.

You might have laughed at my dream, if I'd told you about it then. *That's nice, Michelle,* you might have said to humor me. But this was more than play. I really believed that I could become a top skater like Brian. There was something true about my vision. I could see the dream perfectly, in every detail. I was just a little kid taking skating lessons at a mall near Torrance, California. There were lots of us at the rink. I'm sure I didn't seem any different from the others. But from that day on, I had this spark in me. It made me feel differently about myself and about skating. What had began as fun was becoming a true *love*.

TEST YOUR VISION

Time is the true test of any vision. When I woke up the next morning after watching Brian skate, the spark was still there. And it was still there the next day and the next. Now, many years later, I still feel it, stronger than ever. Once the dream sparked, it kept burning. I had a very, very, *very* long way to go, of course. But the dream was powerful right from the start, and it's stayed with me a very, very, *very* long time.

This is not the kind of dream that you forget when you wake up. It's not some one-night wish like, "If only Leonardo DiCaprio would walk through my front door!" This is the kind of dream that stays alive in you because there's some truth in it. It could come true.

It's important to know the difference. If there's a dream you've had for a while, think back on it. Has it stayed with you every day of every week? Or is it something you only want to do when you see someone else having success with it?

What I'm talking about is the difference between thinking *I'd like to be up on that podium,* and *I want to skate my heart out the way that person does.* If it's just the podium you want, then you may only be dealing with a fantasy.

Even just a tiny speck of truth can keep a dream going. I think I knew even at seven that I could dedicate myself to skating with all my heart the way Brian did. I didn't believe I had any special talent. I could jump and spin okay. But that would only get me so far.

I have no doubt about it: being able to see the kind of skater I want to be has taken me farther than raw talent ever could.

No matter what you're trying to do—play a musical instrument, skate, make the honor roll—if you want to be successful, you have to start with a bright, intricate, wonderful dream. Maybe to everyone else it seems like an impossible dream. The important thing is that it seems possible to *you*. And that time will not make it go away.

It's an old saying, and I think it's really true: *If you can see it, you can achieve it.*

CLIMBING MOUNTAINS

Maybe it's because of where I live, but I like to think of a dream as a beautiful mountain, reaching up into the clouds. Of course, climbing it wouldn't be very exciting if you could get there in one easy step. Any mountain worth scaling will offer you lots of challenges along the way. I've been climbing my mountain since that day when I was seven, and there's still a lot of mountain left to go.

A mountain climber doesn't tackle Mount Everest unless she really loves mountains. And if you don't love your dream, you won't make it up to the top of your mountain either.

It can be a big dream or a little dream. Maybe all

you want is to sing a song in the talent show, or build a tree house. Or maybe you want to be president of the United States! It doesn't matter. You have to want to do it for the right reasons: because you love the dream. I can't imagine working as hard as I do at skating if my heart wasn't completely in it. And never in a million years would I have made it as far as I have.

Not every step up the mountain will be pure delight. Many will be tough. They'll test your belief in your dream. So it's important to ask yourself some questions before you decide which dream to pursue.

First of all, is your dream something you are attracted to? In other words, is the thing you want to do fun for you? You shouldn't have to push and pull and coax to make yourself follow your dream.

Second, is it really *your* dream? Our friends, parents, and teachers are always urging us to do this or that. Usually they want what's best for us, but they don't always know what really lights a spark inside of us. It's up to you to tell them. Don't choose a dream just because someone else is doing it, or because it's something you're supposed to do. Your dream might be to play hockey instead of to decorate doll houses. If so, go for it!

Third, does your dream pass the test of time? Maybe yesterday you dreamed of being a horseback rider, while today you dream of ballet dancing. If you can't choose between them yet, then don't. You're young. Dabble for a while. Have fun. If a time comes when you want to get more serious about one or the other and have to make a choice between the two, sit down and make a list. List the good things and the drawbacks about each dream. That should help make things clearer for you.

And remember, it's never too late to try something totally new. Maybe you've been riding horses and taking ballet lessons since you were four. Then when you're fourteen, you decide to try rock climbing. You discover that's your true passion, not riding or dancing. Don't worry about it. Dreams can change or awaken at any time in your life.

If you pursue the things that interest you the most, your dream might just come to you without your realizing it. Maybe it's something that no one's ever done before, a mountain no one's ever climbed. In which case, you can be the first to reach the top.

VISION'S COUSIN: MOTIVATION

I see little kids training at Ice Castle all the time, and I always wonder, which one will be the next big star? Which one has that spark inside?

Usually it's the kids who get up right away after they fall. The ones whose parents don't have to nag at them to practice. It's not necessarily the ones with the most obvious talent. It's the ones with the most *motivation* of their own. Motivation and vision are very close relatives.

Once you've seen your dream, it will begin to take on a life of its own. With luck, it will grow stronger and stronger. Some days it will be stronger than you. You'll need it, believe me. When you're feeling lazy or blue or things aren't going so great, it'll get you out of bed and out the door. It will *motivate* you to keep going. "Remember me? Your beautiful dream!? *Hello!!??*"

That's what's going on inside the heads of those little kids who fall in practice and get up again. Motivation picks them right up off the ice and gives them a gentle push into the next jump.

You can't force a dream to spark. It has to hit you at just the right moment. Maybe when you're seven, maybe when you're seventeen, maybe later. You might have lots of little dreams, or you might have one big one. Everyone's different that way. If you're lucky, you'll be able to look at everything that you want to achieve as a kind of mountain to climb, whether it's learning an instrument, or running a five-minute mile.

It's amazing to think of all the different things people dream of doing. Things I could never imagine doing myself. Things that have never been done before. Maybe your dream is something you're embarrassed to tell anyone about, because you're afraid they'll laugh or say it's impossible.

Well, don't worry about them. Your dream is between you and your pillow. Close your eyes and see it. Imagine every detail. Does it seem too real not to be true? Now open your eyes. Do you feel that spark in your heart?

If so, then you've already got an extremely important quality that no one can be a champion without. Whatever you want to do, don't be afraid to dream big. If you try to do the impossible, you may end up doing the next-to-impossible. You might not reach your ultimate goal, but at least you've given it your best shot. And that's all that matters.

VISION QUEST(IONS)

If you've got a dream of something you want to do, ask yourself these questions to see if it's real or just a one-night wish:

1) To make it come true, do you need more luck (winning the lottery) than sweat (running a marathon)?

2) Is your dream about fame or fortune (winning an Oscar), or is it about doing something you love (acting, no matter how big or small the role)?

3) Tomorrow morning after your alarm goes off, try to see your dream in every detail. Now: Does it make you want to jump out of bed and attack the day?

4) Make a timeline that shows when (as close as you can recall) your dream was born. Note changes in your dream and things you've done to make it come true since then. Mark today's date, then keep your timeline in a safe place. Take it out every month and note your latest feelings about it.

Answer these questions honestly, and you'll know if you have the stuff that dreams are made of.

CHAPTER TWO

Discipline

O nce you know your dream, it always helps to have some talent for the thing you've chosen. But talent will only take you so far up that mountain. The rest is hard work, and it won't happen without discipline.

Some people are afraid of the word discipline. I hear people say, "I'd like to be a writer (or a gymnast or a biologist). I think I've got some talent, but I'm afraid I don't have the self-discipline."

Maybe we're shy about the word discipline because we associate it with strict rules and chores. I guess it reminds us of punishment. Well, put that attitude out of your head right now. Don't let discipline scare you off! Its bark is worse than its bite. Try to think of it in a whole new way. Think of it as another name for love.

★ ★ ★

DISCIPLINE = LOVE?!

Do you have a dog? There are lots of things you have to do to take care of him. You have to walk him, brush him, feed him and train him. All of that takes discipline. But you do it because you love him. Even if he eats your book report or your favorite shoe, or needs to go out when it's raining, you still take care of him because you love him.

If you didn't take care of him, what would happen to him? If you forgot to feed him one day, would that be okay? No.

Discipline is an every-day thing. Not once a week or twice a week. It's a commitment to something you love. If the love's there, the discipline will come, I promise. If you can develop discipline, it will be your friend, not your enemy. It will take care of you.

I have to be disciplined about everything. Training every day, eating well, getting to bed at a reasonable time, and still making time to relax, all take discipline. And that's on an easy day. Until recently, I had to study for high school, and now I'm going to college while training.

I'm not saying it's easy to be disciplined. Some days the alarm goes off, and I wish I could just hit the snooze button—a two-hour snooze button. I think, Maybe I'll take today off. But then I argue with myself: No, you won't! Oh, yeah?!

Then, without fail, something pushes me out of bed. I don't mean my parents or my coach. It's something in *me* that does it. Because I have the motivation I told you about, I've also got discipline. After all these years, I've actually got lots of it now. But it has taken time. It didn't happen overnight.

It can be difficult to get motivated when you're starting something new. When Karen and I first started practicing early in the morning, before school, it wasn't easy. We did everything we could to make it hurt less. To get a few extra minutes of sleep, we slept in our tights so all we had to do was roll out of bed when the alarm went off. I'd look at the ice in the rink, shiver, and say to myself, "Why am I doing this again?"

Pretty soon, though, I'd be skating. And that was all the reminder I needed. Eventually, I got used to it, and before long it was a part of my life that I loved. In fact, skating early in the morning when there aren't a lot of people around is magical.

Sometimes at the start you just have to force yourself to be disciplined. There's no way around it. We all think that discipline will hurt us, at first. It takes a while to figure out that it's not as bad as we thought it would be. You need a new attitude. Think of it as love, not punishment.

If you're doing something you really love, you'll look forward to doing it. You won't have to drag yourself, kicking and screaming. You'll simply do it, without arguing with yourself, because you won't want to miss out on a day of it. Trust me.

DISCIPLINE'S COUSINS

Showing up is half the battle. That's what discipline means: you get out of bed, get to the library, open your books. Already you're a success!

Next, you have to make sure *all* of you has shown up—your mind as well as your body. If my mind wanders during practice, my coach, Frank, will say, "Earth to Michelle!" and snap me out of it. If I'm still spaced out, he'll end that day's practice altogether: why waste both his time and mine? There's a big difference between being there and *being there*.

That happens rarely, though. By now I don't wander off much. Once I'm there, I'm there. I'm not thinking about the movie I saw last night or what I'm going to have for dinner. I'm focused on what I'm doing *now*. *Focus* and *attention* are first cousins to discipline.

Once I start, I don't want to stop. Even if I'm tired, I feel like I can always do a little bit more. *A little bit more, a little bit more*. I've said those words to myself so many times in my life. *Just do this one more* time—*then one more time—then one more time.* Suddenly you'll find yourself reaching a whole new level.

You'll find these little bits not just in the activity you practice, but all around in your life. Everything you do affects your ability to accomplish your dream. If you can be disciplined there, too, it will help you climb your mountain. Here are some of the little things you can do to build discipline:

★ Be on time.

★ Follow the program you've laid out diligently.

★ Be reliable: if you say you're going to do something, do it.

★ Keep your room clean: Hmm, you might have heard this one before, but it's true—being organized makes being disciplined so much easier.

Just think in little bits like this. A little bit of effort on top of a lot of other little bits . . . and suddenly you're halfway up your mountain.

DISCIPLINE'S EVIL TWIN: PRESSURE

Many of the qualities that I'm going to tell you about have their bad side, if you overdo them. Just like they have good cousins, they also have evil twins.

My dad has always told me, "There's a fine line between discipline and pressure." There is such a thing as over-disciplining yourself. If you push it too much, you can start to feel pressure. Pressure leads to overwork, and overworking yourself is not productive.

Usually your body or mind tells you when you're getting overworked. It starts to hurt, or you can't think straight, or you become irritable. Everyone needs to take a break at some point. For some people that's harder to do than getting started.

I'll tell you more about how to deal with pressure in chapter eight. Usually it's not a big problem when you're just starting out. But if you do feel like you're starting to get stressed out, then don't feel bad about letting up for a little while.

There's something else that can happen once you get going in a routine that works for you. You may enjoy it for a time, and then suddenly find it's getting hard again. But we'll talk about that later. That's when you'll need dedication.

DISCIPLINE QUIZ

1) Does it look like a tornado just hit your bedroom?
 a) no, winds are calm
 b) yes, a class V

2) When your teacher's giving a lecture, how long does your mind stand at attention? Rank yourself:
 a) the whole period: General
 b) 3/4 of the period: Captain
 c) 1/2 the period: Sergeant
 d) 1/2 a second: Space Cadet

3) You want to wear your favorite dress. You get it from:
 a) your closet, where it's hanging neatly
 b) the floor of your closet, underneath your sneakers
 c) the clothes pile on your floor
 d) you don't have a clue where it is

4) When your mom says turn off the TV and do your homework, you reply:
 a) It's already done
 b) I'm doing it during the commercials
 c) I'll get to it as soon as this video is over
 d) I can do it tomorrow on the bus

If you answered **a** to all the questions, you've got discipline to spare.

CHAPTER THREE

Perseverance

THE LAWS OF FLAWS

If you take what you do as seriously as I take skating, then you're going to learn a lot about yourself. The good and the bad. Your strengths and your weaknesses. And very early on, you'll learn something very important about yourself: you're not perfect.

Well, you might as well accept it. You'll *never* be perfect. Nobody is.

In the beginning, your imperfections may seem huge. Your first attempt at a French accent will sound like a cat being strangled. When you're learning any new skill you're bound to make lots of mistakes. Just try not to get frustrated. In life, everyone falls at some point. I've fallen literally thousands of times, and there will be times when you'll fall as well. But that's okay. You just have to keep getting back up again. If you have the ability to *persevere*, eventually you'll turn those giant flaws into distant memories!

When I was five years old, the first skating lesson I learned was: how to fall. My instructor was wise. He knew that until I learned to fall, I couldn't learn how *not* to fall. You see? Your mistakes will be your best friends if you let them teach you.

Luckily, being a perfect person isn't a requirement for success of any kind. But being honest about your weaknesses is. There's no way around it: if you want to do anything right, you first have to figure out what you're doing wrong. That means making lots of mistakes—and learning to accept and understand them.

LISTEN TO CRITICISM

Of course, if you want to correct your flaws, you have to be able to take criticism. Doing anything well is very hard work. But it's so much harder if you try to do it all on your own. I certainly couldn't skate as well as I do if I tried to hide my flaws from people who can help me fix them.

Before you even begin a new task, you probably have some idea in your head of how you're going to do it. You can hear your voice hitting every note of "I Feel Pretty" perfectly. Unfortunately, it probably won't take you very long to learn that you've got it all wrong.

But if doing that thing well is more important to you than being right, then you'll be in great shape. You have to listen to the people around you who have a little more experience—a teacher, coach, parent, or friend. You have to take a little criticism.

I'm making it sound easier than it is, I know. Taking criticism sometimes requires more courage than doing a new jump. But if you want to believe people when they say you're doing great, then you have to be able to listen when they tell you what you're doing wrong.

It can be hard to ask for help sometimes. But try it and you'll be glad. In school, for instance, if you're having a hard time in math, do you hate to ask for help? Do you want to try out for the school play but you're too embarrassed to ask someone to help you with your audition? Well, stop that! If you really want something, you have to want it enough to ask for help.

I've seen kids who won't listen to anyone. They seem to think they know it all already. Well, I never would have gotten out of the little mall rink where I started skating if I didn't listen to my coaches, my parents, my brother, Ron, and my sister, Karen.

To succeed, you need to believe in yourself. But you also need to respect the people who know more than you. If you want to improve at what you're doing, you ought to consider yourself lucky if someone you trust is willing to help you and be honest with you, the way Frank was with me after the '98 Olympics.

At the same time, it's also true that not all teachers are perfect. Sometimes you don't have good chemistry with an instructor. And sometimes people can be really hard on you. If that happens, try not to take it personally. And don't just *take* it either. If you think you're not getting good criticism, get a second opinion. Talk to your teammates or another teacher or your parents. It's still about listening—especially to yourself—but it's also about developing selective hearing.

My family has a tradition. Every year our parents sit down with us and tell us what our weaknesses are. This is an important time, when they're honest with us, and we have to be honest with ourselves.

Most people can't believe it when I tell them about this tradition. I suppose you do have to be careful when you're pointing out someone's weaknesses. First of all, they have to want to hear them. Secondly, you have to be sure you're doing it for the right reasons—to help, not to hurt.

I'm not saying all families should do this. I'm only saying that in my family it works. If my dad forgets to do it, I miss it. I can take criticism. It's when I *don't* get any that I worry.

I'M NOT PERFECT, AND NEITHER ARE YOU

Frank is one of the best coaches in the world. The first time I had a lesson with him, when I was about eleven, I was so nervous. I got on the ice, started my program, and quickly fell—*splat*. I was so embarrassed that I just sat there.

"Get up, young lady!" Frank insisted. "Keep going!"

The first thing I learned from Frank was that when you fall, you don't sit there and cry about it. You use it as an opportunity to learn something. I've been falling in front of Frank ever since, and each time I do I discover something new.

It's great to strive for perfection. But if you carve a certain picture in stone and don't allow it to change or be influenced by other people, you only hold yourself back. There's an old saying: *The perfect is the enemy of the good.* Don't let perfection be your master. If you let it rule you too strictly, it could ruin everything, even your chance to be good at what you do.

Moments of near-perfection do happen every once in a while, though, and when they do they're a kind of bonus, a miracle born out of your love of what you're doing. They're a direct result of all those mistakes you made at the beginning, and all that criticism you listened to. You've simply got to let yourself make them.

When I make a mistake during a competition, the judges take points off my score, so I try not to do my falling there. However, I can't be careful or cautious. The only way to do a triple/triple jump combination is to go all-out, and that means there's a chance I could fall.

So practice is where I try to figure out how far out all-out is. I try to get all the real bad jumps out of the way before the competition, and I spend a lot of quality time up close and personal with the ice.

Frank doesn't have to tell me to get up anymore. Now there's a voice in my head that gets me on my feet in a heartbeat. Believe me, I don't want to dwell on a fall. I want to learn from it, then put it behind me as quickly as possible so I can work on getting it right.

FORGIVE BUT DON'T FORGET

Regret is a terrible word. I think maybe it's my least favorite word in the language. Try not to spend time regretting your mistakes. Don't think you're a bad person because you got a B on a test instead of an A, or because you accidentally hurt your best friend's feelings. If you find that you're dwelling on your weaknesses instead of letting them show you how to improve, maybe you need to ease up a bit.

Be tough on yourself, but not hard or cruel. And don't let anyone be cruel to you.

If regret is a terrible word, forgiveness is a great one. If someone makes a mistake—let's say your best friend hurts your feelings—you shouldn't just get mad at her, but try to understand how it happened. It's the same with your own mistakes. You have to make an effort to understand how they happened, and then forgive yourself.

Forgive, but don't forget: learn from the mistake.

My performance at the National Championships in 1997 was one of the most disappointing moments of my life. I was heavily favored to win, yet I fell not once but twice, in front of millions of people.

But it wasn't the end of the world. I thought to myself, It's not like I did something so terrible. I just fell. It happens. Now, I'm actually really grateful for what I learned from those falls. Without them, I might not have made the leap I made the following year, when I took my skating to a whole new level.

There's another quote I love. It's from *Walden*, which was written by Henry Thoreau. He said, "The fault-finder will find fault even in paradise." In other words, if perfection is the only thing that will make you happy, then you'll never be happy. So think about how you treat your mistakes. If you can make them work for you, it's a lesson you'll be able to use for the rest of your life.

TEST YOUR PERSEVERANCE

1) If you fall off a horse, do you:
  a) get back up again
  b) stay on the ground?

2) If your sister doesn't like the pea-green sweater you gave her, do you:
  a) offer to exchange it
  b) burst into tears because obviously you're the worst sister in the world?

3) If your teacher comments that your paper on the American Revolution is interesting, but the revolution was actually about freedom, not tea, do you:
  a) go back over your research
  b) transfer to a new school because the teachers here don't know a thing about history?

4) When you stub your toe against a wall, do you
  a) decide to look where you're going next time
  b) blame the wall?

5) If you get a 98 on a math test, do you
  a) pat yourself on the back for a job well done
  b) beg your teacher to let you take it over again —you've just got to have that 100?!

If you answered **a**, you have a high degree of perseverance.

CHAPTER FOUR

Dedication

W hen I first learned to skate, it was so simple! I was thrilled to stand up on the ice without falling. Pretty soon I was gliding faster, doing some simple jumps and spins, and I thought to myself: I'm a skater!

But the more I learned, the more I saw that there was still so much to learn. It's like when you're on that mountain: you're climbing up to a ridge that you've been looking at for half the day, telling yourself, "If I can just make it to the top, I'll be happy." Then you get there only to see the rest of the mountain and how much farther you have to go.

To make it any higher now, you'll need dedication.

To dedicate means "to name or set aside." When you dedicate a poem or a picture to someone, you're setting it apart as something special, in that person's spirit or memory. You have to do the same thing with the activity you've chosen to pursue. There comes a point where you have to ask yourself: Am I going to make a commitment to this? Am I going to set aside the time, energy, and other things I'll miss out on to be really *dedicated*?

DEDICATION'S COUSINS: DETERMINATION, DEVOTION, AND COMMITMENT

I found out about dedication in 1992, when I moved up to Lake Arrowhead to work at Ice Castle. For the first time, I saw how determined the top-level skaters were. They didn't just concentrate on the jumps and the spins, but also on all the little things: the way they held their heads, hands, and arms, the way they moved to the music. I could see how determined they were to skate beautifully.

Determination and dedication work together. You know what it feels like when you're determined, even if it's just to get your favorite sweater from the top shelf of your closet. You won't let anything stand in your way. You'll do whatever it takes and think up new solutions to obstacles. You get very creative when you're determined. Suddenly you find that you're willing to work extremely hard. Harder, maybe, than you ever imagined you could.

Let's say you take up ballet. At first you do well. Your teacher says you've got natural talent, and you're having fun. You move into more advanced classes, and it gets harder. You still have fun doing the dance combinations, but you make a few mistakes. The teacher criticizes you because your arms are slightly wrong, your feet slightly wrong. Do you get annoyed when she focuses on tiny things? Or do you keep going, trying to learn as much as you can because you're devoted to the art?

Devotion and *commitment* are also cousins of dedication. When you devote yourself to something, you're saying you're going to give your all. You're making the commitment. Not excuses. Excuses like *if only it wasn't so hot!* or *it's raining!* are just ways of avoiding dedication.

LOVE THE DETAILS

It's important to dream big, but it's just as important to love the small gains that you make. When I decided my dream was to go to the Olympics, I then took a good look at what it would take to get there, and set smaller goals for myself that would lead the way. I would keep breaking down my larger goals into smaller ones. Eventually, I achieved my big dream by achieving all the little ones that came first.

It takes a thousand tiny steps to climb a mountain. The secret is not to complain about how many steps there are, but to enjoy each and every one.

Being dedicated means that every little detail counts. You have to *love* them all. When I started working with Frank, there were a million bad habits I had to give up, and a million little things I had to become aware of. I suddenly had to use parts of my body I never knew existed. I was skating from the bottom of my skates to the top of my head.

I could write a book about the things I had to teach my feet alone! I always had to point my toes. And I had to work especially hard on my "edges," the way the blades of my skates carved the ice.

That was just the beginning. My bearing, poise, the position of my hands (the slightest movement can make the difference between artistic and awkward), the way I moved over the ice—these are things only the most keen observer would notice. They're almost invisible, but paying attention to them is what dedication is all about. Without them, I never would have been more than a cute jumping bean.

FOCUS

When you focus on the details, it's like you're making the tiny brush strokes of a painting, the ones that make it come to life. You have to love the details as much as you love the big picture, your vision.

Athletes use the word focus a lot. I think this is what focus is: it's seeing the little picture and the big picture at the same time. It's zooming in on the details, giving each one the respect and love it deserves. At the same time in the back of your mind, you let your vision organize them into the big picture you want to paint. It's hard to do, and only by dedicating yourself to the details can it happen.

KNOW THE HISTORY

Finding my focus and dedication to skating was all a part of gaining a deeper understanding of the sport. You'll need to find this too, whether you're playing a sport or playing the piano or writing poems. But if you want to fully understand anything, you should know the rules and traditions inside out, and that means studying the history of those who came before you.

You can't be a physicist if you don't study Einstein. If you decide to become a painter, you'll need to study the masters: Rubens, Van Gogh, Picasso, to name a few. Or maybe you want to be a better sister. Then the best people to look to could be your parents or your grandparents.

Sometimes, too, by looking at the past, you'll find something wonderful that everyone else has forgotten about. Then you can make it new again. You've probably been hearing a lot of swing music on the radio lately by bands like Big Bad Voodoo Daddy. That music was popular when our grandparents were young, but today's musicians have rediscovered it and made it fun and new again.

I like to do that, too. I put a new type of spiral in my routine called a Charlotte spiral. It's the move where I'm moving backwards in my spiral and I lean forward so my hand touches the ice. But this step isn't actually new. I saw it on one of Frank's old films and we decided to add it to my routine.

Some of the skaters I admire most, like Peggy Fleming and Dorothy Hamill, competed before I was born. But I've learned so much by watching films of them. The sport wasn't invented out of thin air, you know. Each innovation and each step of progress was won with a lot of hard work and sacrifice.

If you can see how the greats before you added a new wrinkle to your discipline, some day you may be the one to add the next new wrinkle. Then you'll be the one that everybody remembers.

Most of all, studying skaters like Peggy and Dorothy and Brian Boitano has shown me how much more there is to love about this sport, and what heights dedication can lead you to.

Of course, like most of the qualities you'll need to succeed, dedication has an evil twin: it's forcing yourself to do something you don't enjoy. Sometimes others put pressure on us. Sometimes we put the pressure on ourselves.

To me, dedication, like all of the qualities I list in this book, boils down to love. You can't devote yourself to something you don't love. So if you find that you're putting in the discipline and the hard work, but the spark isn't there, please don't torture yourself over it. Take some time to have fun, think, and read. That's how you'll discover the things you really love.

Some day, though, I hope you'll find something to dedicate yourself to. When you do, you'll find that the dedication you bring to it will find its way into other parts of your life.

Everything that I do, I try to do as well as I can. My schoolwork, my friends, my family—I try to give them the same focused attention. I'm a dedicated person, not just a dedicated athlete.

QUIZ: ARE YOU BRINGING DEDICATION TO YOUR SPORT OR ART OR OTHER ACTIVITY?

1) When you meet others who are more advanced than you, do you carefully observe everything they do?

2) Can you name three people who were great at it?

3) Have you read at least two books about it?

4) When you have to stop, can you hardly wait to get back to it?

If you answered yes to all four, then congratulations: you're on your way to having dedication.

CHAPTER FIVE

Courage

If you've never taken a skating lesson, you may think that what I do on the ice is impossible. Maybe it seems like I've got something that you don't have—a built-in gyroscope (a device that keeps a spinning object stable) or something.

Well, believe me, I don't. When I was starting out, I couldn't do any of those jumps and spins. Over the years, some of them have come more easily than others. But for each of them there was a first time: a time when I had to try something I'd never done before, and believe I could pull it off. A time when, more than anything else, I needed a little courage.

First steps are scary for everybody. When you make your first dive from the high board, or give your first speech in front of the class, or ride a chair lift for the first time—all of these require courage.

Courage has two twins: *faith* and *confidence*.

Maybe you don't think you have all three, but I bet if you look hard enough, you'll find that you have at least one of them. If you let them, they'll help you get through your first step and your second step and all the way up your mountain.

I'll tell you a secret: it's the *faith* and *confidence* inside of me (not a gyroscope!) that make all those impossible moves I do seem easy.

HAVE A LITTLE FAITH

I've been trying to do a triple axel for years. It's really hard, because when you do an axel, you start the jump facing forward and end facing backward. That means in a single motion you're actually rotating one-and-a-half times around. So in a triple axel, you have to rotate your body in the air three-and-a-half times and then land perfectly on one foot.

I can't do it—yet. Most of the top-level men can, but only a couple of women have even attempted one in competition. Sometimes, to be honest, it seems impossible.

But I haven't given up. I don't work on it all the time, but it's there in the back of my mind, teasing me. Even though I still can't quite picture what my body needs to do to make it happen, I know for a matter of fact—or is it a matter of faith?—that there's a way.

The reason I know this is that there was a time, not so long ago, when women weren't even doing *double* axels. Every year, in every endeavor humanly possible, people are breaking through barriers that once seemed fixed. It's a fact of life that you don't know what you're capable of until you try.

Being a beginner at something can be the most exciting time. If you have a little talent and a lot of dedication, you improve so fast! But eventually you reach a point where the training gets more difficult, and you need something else. When all else fails, you've got to have a little faith in yourself.

Faith means believing in something you can't see, because it's not there yet. Believing in potential. Everyone—and I mean *everyone*—has potential that they can't see. Faith can help you turn potential into reality.

That's how we've gotten as far as we have. Back when doing a double axel seemed like an impossible feat, a few women believed it could be done. I take some of my faith from them. My courage is built on their courage.

Here's another old saying. Like the others, it hasn't survived this long for nothing: *Where there's a will, there's a way.*

I have good rule of thumb to go along with it: *If you get a powerful notion to do something, even if you can't imagine how you'll do it, it's possible.* Have faith!

THE CONFIDENCE FACTOR

After I fell (and fell) in the '97 Nationals, Brian Boitano called me up and gave me some great advice about confidence. He said: *Your problem is that you're thinking negatively. When you approach a jump, you're thinking about all the things that could go wrong. You need to turn off that negative voice. Instead, you need simply to tell yourself what you have to do to make the jump right.*

I knew immediately that he was right. I was *psyching myself out.* Somewhere along the way, I'd lost my confidence. It's strange how it can slip out on you just when you're not looking.

Now, it's one thing to say, *Have confidence.* But it's another thing to *be* confident. It's not like snapping your fingers. You can't always just switch it on or off. If it was so easy to be confident, no one would ever get nervous or make a silly mistake.

That's why Brian's advice was so good. He didn't just say, *Be confident.* He showed me how to do it. When you think negatively, like I was doing, you let bad things happen to you. But if you follow Brian's advice and think *positively*—no matter what it is you're trying to do—then you're the boss. You're in charge of yourself. And you're on the road to being confident.

Brian's advice is useful in so many situations. Let's say you're giving a speech in class. Most people would be nervous, of course. Waiting for your turn, you might be tempted to worry about all the things that could go wrong. *What if I lose my place? Drop my index cards? What if my voice cracks . . . !?*

If you think that way, you can almost count on jumbling up your words. Your voice won't come out loudly or clearly enough. You'll seem afraid up there. You'll make silly mistakes. You'll make giving a speech look hard to do.

Everyone gets nervous. Nerves can be useful. They give you a lot of energy before you have to perform. But you can use that energy to think negatively or you can use it to think positively. Instead of thinking about all that can go wrong in your speech, try to focus on some of the things you can actually do to make it right. Not too many—just one or two. But try to put everything else out of your mind. Tell yourself before it's your turn, *Stand up straight. Remember to breathe.* Or tell yourself something that Frank likes to tell me before I skate: *Don't defend, attack!*

Then get up there and take charge of yourself. Everyone will think it's easy for you. *That's* what being confident is.

★ ★ ★

39

TAKING CHARGE

I know that when you're starting out, it's easy to be full of doubt. You might not feel strong enough or big enough to do the things you want. You probably think that kids who are older than you have all the confidence in the world—they seem smarter, faster, more coordinated.

Well, the truth is that even as you get older, it's easy to have doubts about yourself. Everything is changing so quickly that you wonder who you are and where you fit in. You may be a little smarter, faster and bigger than you were a couple years ago, but inside you still feel like a little kid. It can take a while for your confidence to catch up with you. You look at little kids swinging upside down from jungle gyms, tumbling all over the place, and saying the very first thing that pops into their heads, and you think: Was I ever that brave?

Yes. You were. And you still are. Everybody has at least a tiny kernel of courage in them. Usually, if you find something that you love to do, that love will work on that little kernel. It will coax the kernel out of you and make it grow.

Here are a few ways that you can exercise and strengthen your courage along the way:

★ Start at the bottom and work your way up. That means start with easy tasks you know you can succeed at before you tackle the harder ones. This way, your confidence and momentum will build. It's like giving your self a running start. Trying to tackle the hard ones before you tackle the easy ones would be going backward.

★ Focus on the positive: concentrate on doing things right. Block out images of doing things wrong. If you're going to do a dive, picture the dive exactly as you want it to be. Block out images of yourself belly-flopping.

★ Commit: if you're going to do something, don't do it halfheartedly. Walk up to that diving board as if you can't wait to get there. As if there's no place in the world you'd rather be.

★ If your confidence feels shaky, talk with someone you respect and who knows you well. They should be able to remind you of your strong points. Then: believe them!

★ Remember your successes. Take an experience or accomplishment that you're proud of and hold it in your memory like a touchstone. When you feel your confidence wavering, take the memory out and touch it. Let it remind you of what you're capable of.

★ Don't sit around and mope: get up and do something, anything, that you enjoy and you're good at. This will change your mind-set (even your brain chemistry!), and get you back on track.

★ Face your fears: If you're afraid of something, try to face it squarely. Don't avoid it, but examine it and think about it. Nine times out of ten, you'll realize there are ways to overcome your fear.

★ If your friends tell you that you're becoming arrogant or stuck-up, listen to them. Confidence does have an evil twin. It's called vanity. True confidence doesn't mean putting people down or acting like you're better than everyone else.

HOW'S YOUR COURAGE QUOTIENT?

1) Raising your hand in class when you think you know the answer but aren't completely sure takes:
   a) courage   **b)** faith
   c) confidence   **d)** insanity

2) When you're learning a new skill you've never tried before, do you say:
   a) Let me at it!   **b)** I'll do my best
   c) It's worth a try   **d)** Get me out of here!

3) When it's your turn to give an oral report, which thought goes through your head as you walk to the front of the class (no matter how nervous you are):
   a) "I'm going to ace this."
   b) "This could be fun."
   c) "Stand up straight and remember to breathe."
   d) "I'm doomed!"

If you answered **d** to the above questions, then you haven't found your courage yet. But keep at it, and you will.

CHAPTER SIX

Peace of Mind

When I'm out there on the ice, all you see is me. That's why they call skating an "individual" sport. But the term is misleading. It might seem like I'm so brave that I don't need anybody. What you don't know is that only part of that courage comes from me. The rest comes from the people who love me.

Above all, my family gives me peace of mind. They take a lot of the pressure and worries off me. I can count on every one of them for anything. They're honest with me. They give me encouragement. They know how to make me laugh. My home is happy and warm and more or less normal. I'm very lucky that way, because I know not everyone has this.

After a long tiring day or a tough competition, I sometimes feel empty and exhausted, like I don't even know who I am. But then I see, for instance, my mom or dad. They say, "Michelle!" and throw their arms around me. They don't have to say or do any more than that. Suddenly I've found myself again.

Everybody needs a place where they feel safe. Whether you're training for the Olympics or writing a report for school, it's that much harder to be successful if you don't have a safe, quiet place to study or practice.

This place is different for everybody. You might not be as lucky as I am, with your family. They might not understand you, or might have some serious problems of their own. So your place might not be at home. Sometimes it's at a friend's house. Or at school in the library or band room or computer room. Or maybe it's at a ballet studio.

Wherever you can find peace of mind, take it. If there's a place where you can be completely yourself and at ease, then go there as much as possible.

THE BARE NECESSITIES

The qualities I've listed in this book are mostly things you need to find inside yourself in order to give yourself the best chance to succeed. But this chapter's a little different. It's about strength you can gain if you nurture relationships outside of yourself.

You'll notice that I didn't write a chapter called "Lots of Money" or "Incredible Beauty" or "Perfect Teeth." Those are nice qualities, and if you have them I hope you enjoy them. But they're certainly not a requirement for success.

I don't know many skaters who come from wealthy families. When I was a kid, we had hardly any money. My parents worked overtime to help our skating dreams come true. The one thing that we could count on in life was each other. And that was a lot.

You can do incredibly great things without a lot of money. But nobody can succeed all on their own. Even if you have all the vision, discipline, courage, and dedication in the world, you can't be an island. You'll be missing something enormous in your life if you shut out people who care about you. They're a necessity of life. Along with the qualities you'll need to find in yourself, they're what will carry you through.

If you have nothing in life but a great friend, you're rich. And you're a winner.

You'll always need a friend who can help you keep your life in perspective and be honest with you. For some people that's a classmate, special teacher, or a coach, or a parent, or even a friend's parent. It's whomever you feel comfortable around. Someone you trust.

If you've started climbing up a mountain and it's taking up a lot of your time, try not to shut out your friends. Don't push them away. You'll need their support through the good times and the bad, and I'm sure they'll need you, too.

Don't neglect your family or your friends. They're the best support group you could ever ask for. While you're working on your part in the school play, don't forget to keep working at those relationships, too. If you'll let them, they'll be a part of your success in so many ways you won't even know how to count them. When you step out onto the stage, you'll be so much bigger than just yourself. You'll have more than just your own faith. You'll have your friends' faith, too.

WHEN THINGS FALL APART

Sometimes things just fall apart. You fail a test. You don't make the team. You have a fight with your best friend, or she moves away. You don't get along with your family, or your teacher.

Or between school and all your activities, your life feels so busy that you're going to burst. You become a kind of robot. You feel like you don't have control over anything anymore—you're just pushing buttons.

Sometimes all the evil twins come out to

play. You're not just disciplined, you're overworked. You're not just persevering, you're overdoing it. You're not confident, you're just stuck-up. That's when you'll really need a peaceful place to go, or someone you can talk to.

When you're down or discouraged, is there someone or something that never fails to cheer you up? Writing in your journal, playing with a pet, reading a favorite book? Relaxing with friends? Listening to music in your room?

If things get really bad and you have a hard time finding someone to talk to, go to a counselor at your school. Most schools have them, and you'd be amazed at how much just talking to them can help. Or you might want to seek out your minister, priest, or rabbi, or a favorite teacher, or a friend's parent.

I like to pick up the phone and call Karen at college. Or curl up with my mom on the sofa and watch TV. Or go shopping. Everyone needs an oasis somewhere. If you're feeling stressed out or sad, there's probably a good reason for it. Sometimes the only way to find the reason is to step away from the problem, as far away as you can get, so you can see it clearly.

The best place to go is wherever you feel most at ease and most yourself, where you don't have to pretend to be something you're not. If you need to cry, you can cry. If you need to laugh, you can laugh.

If you have a place like that—friends like that, a family like that—then whatever you do, don't take it for granted! It's as precious as anything in your life. It's probably the first key to your health, both mental and physical.

Incredible Beauty, Perfect Teeth, and Lots of Money will only take you so far. But if you have peace of mind, you have one of the biggest secrets to success of all.

WANT TO FIND SOME PEACE OF MIND? TRY TO THINK OF:

1) Someone who makes you laugh and feel totally at ease.

2) Something you like to do that always makes you happy.

3) A place where you feel safe, relaxed, and able to be yourself.

4) A book or poem that you love.

5) A parent, counselor, teacher, coach, or other adult whom you trust.

Every time you look at your list, you'll know just how successful you are.

CHAPTER SEVEN

Flexibility

O ne thing you should know about life is that
as soon as you think you've got it all figured
out, something will change and force you to
figure things out all over again. Sorry—maybe I
should have mentioned this at the beginning!

In fact, just about the only thing that stays the
same is the way things always change. This is especially true when you're young. Your body will grow
and change. Your mind will learn and evolve. Just
when you think you know everything, you discover
something new. Your abilities will develop and your
interests will shift. You need to be very flexible to
handle all of it.

If you could take a time-lapse picture of yourself
and see the change that's happened to you over the
past year, I bet you'd be amazed. Even if your height
didn't change, you'd see lots of little things: your

face, your posture, your hair, the way you dress . . .

Change is like a wave, and you're like a surfer. There's no point fighting it—you have to ride the wave. Let it carry you along and look at the ride as an adventure. Change can even lead you out of bad times and solve some of your problems for you. If you're having trouble with friends, or brothers or sisters, and it seems like nothing you do makes it better, remember, nothing stays the same forever. You'll change, they'll change, and pretty soon the world will look completely different to you.

ADAPT AND GROW

No one can predict the future. You can't really be ready for the amount of growth that's coming your way. But if you can be flexible, and try not to get stuck in your ways, you can adapt to it. Probably every month there's some new thing you need to adapt to—some strange twist of events or some weird snarl in your thread. Your own body and skills will be changing constantly.

I grew four inches between the age of eleven and twelve. When you're a skater and everything depends on your balance and the height of your jumps, that's a pretty big adjustment to make! But I learned to deal with it. Actually, the change was more overwhelming to other people than it was to me. That's because I adapted to my changing body day by day. Four inches may sound like a lot, but if you spread it out over 365 days, and you're adapting to it each of those days, then it's really not such a big deal.

My body kept changing all through my teens, and people always seemed to worry that I wouldn't be able to handle it. They thought I'd topple over, or something. Some people seemed to think that my skating career would be over with puberty. What they couldn't know about me was that while my body was changing and getting stronger, so was my mind.

At the 1995 World Championships in Birmingham, England, I was only fourteen years old. I looked like a baby compared to most of the other skaters there. My hair was in a ponytail, and I didn't have any makeup on. But the look on my face must have been very serious when I took the ice, because just before I started to skate, Frank said one word: "Sparkle!"

Something about that word relaxed me and made me feel like it was okay to enjoy just being there. I sparkled all over that rink and skated the best program of my life. I landed seven triple jumps, more than any other skater. I was so thrilled! I only finished fourth, but I didn't care.

I couldn't have skated any better that night, so I was happy with my performance. But I knew to improve my skating I would have to make some changes.

I realized I needed to develop a whole new dimension as a skater. Technically I was very good, but as an *artist* I had a lot of growing to do. I dedicated myself to that, and the following year I unveiled a whole new program: I skated as Salome, who did the dance of the seven veils in the famous Bible story.

I showed up at the first competition of the season a different person. I was older. For the first time I wore makeup while skating. My costume was very dramatic and grown-up.

People who hadn't seen me for a while were shocked to see the change. But to me it was fun, and it felt natural. My mind and emotions had been evolving right along with my body. I'd already adapted to the change. The public would just have to adapt to it too, eventually.

Sometimes it's harder for the people around you—parents, teachers, grandparents—to let you grow up than it is for you yourself. They love you the way you are and want to keep you that way. People seemed to like the cute little Michelle. But only my family, my coach, my closest friends, and I knew the real me. No one else had any way of knowing that I had the kind of dedication, or ability, to become a more mature skater. I couldn't expect them to know. It only mattered that *I* knew.

Now look at me. I'm a completely different skater than I was then. Now I'm considered an "artistic" skater. Every year we change the whole concept of my programs, and that keeps me sharp and flexible both in mind and body.

Sometimes, you see, change happens to you whether or not you want it to. And sometimes it won't happen unless you let it happen.

DON'T BE AFRAID TO LET GO

After the '95 Worlds, I got more change than I bargained for. The hard part wasn't adjusting my skating style, it was adapting my sense of who I was.

Adapting my life—my daily drills, habits, rituals and routines—to the new me was hard, too. Routines can be great, but you need to examine them every so often and make sure you're not getting into a rut. If they're not working for you, then don't be afraid to leave them behind. All of us have to let go of things as we grow up. If you're going to adapt to your changes, then you'll need to be open to new ideas and new wrinkles.

Sometimes change comes in unexpected ways.

You might discover that your real talent lies in a different direction than you first thought. Let's say you play forward on your soccer team, and one day the goalie is sick and you have to fill in for her. Suddenly you find out you've got great hands, and guarding the goal is your real talent.

Don't be afraid to adjust your vision and change your dream. Just because you've always imagined yourself scoring the winning goal doesn't mean your dream can't change. Let a new dream come into focus. See yourself *saving* the winning goal from being scored. Feel a new spark?

If you're feeling down or stuck, maybe what you need to do is make a little change. It doesn't have to be major. It can even be a little thing. All my life I had long hair. First the ponytail. Then the sophisticated bun. It was totally part of who I was and how I saw myself. Then one day I cut it all off. And what did I find? An exciting discovery: Michelle is not her hair! If you look at my hair, you'll see a new me. But if you look in my eyes, you'll see the *real* me.

EMBRACE THE ADVENTURE

If adapting to change sounds like a challenge—it is! But it's also an adventure. Every day, as you change, you discover something new about yourself and your potential.

Some things, like your eyes, won't change. Your friends will always see the real you. But at the same time, the real you is always changing. Think about this for a minute: who was your favorite singer a year ago? Two years ago? And who is it now? There's probably a different answer for each year. But didn't you feel, each time, *I'll always love that singer the best. I'll always be loyal.*

We want happy times to stay forever. But letting things change, and adapting to change, is how we get to know our real selves as we grow up. We're not one fixed thing.

Let change happen. Be like a surfer riding a wave. Don't fight it. Fighting change is just being stubborn. A surfer has to bend and lean and twist in all kinds of ways just to stay on her board. Try to feel where the wave is going. Let it carry you to new places. And embrace the adventure of it all.

MEASURE YOUR CHANGES

See how much you've changed already by making a time-lapse picture of yourself:

1) Write down the name of your favorite singer for every year going as far back as you can remember.

2) Write down three or four of your favorite books for every year going as far back as you can remember.

3) Look at pictures of yourself from the time you were a baby until now. Pick one for every age and lay them out in a row.

4) If you keep a diary or a journal, read the earliest entry. Then open it at random and read pages from other times in your life.

Now, look at the changing picture you've painted of yourself. Notice all the flexibility it's taken to adapt to all those changes!

CHAPTER EIGHT

Patience

The change I decided to make when I was fourteen didn't come overnight, though I wished it could have. Making up your mind to do something is just the first step. In between you and your dream are lots of little steps you're going to have to take.

Occasionally you'll feel like things aren't going fast enough for you. But there's really nothing you can do about it. Sometimes you're ready for change before change is ready for you. The only thing that will help you then is patience.

You can't get to the top of the mountain in one giant leap. So relax and start taking those little steps. Once you begin achieving small goals, you'll start believing more in the big ones.

Discipline, dedication, confidence, flexibility— all these qualities will take you a long way in your quest up your mountain. But sometimes the right thing to do is . . . nothing.

HURRY UP AND WAIT

It's pretty funny that I'm giving you advice about how to be patient, because I'm one of the most impatient people I know. Patience is a quality I've really had to work hard at. From the moment I started to skate, I've wanted to push ahead to the next thing and the next. My motto after learning a new move was, *Okay. Got that. Next!*

If one of the lessons of Birmingham was that I needed to make some big changes in my life, the other was that I had to be patient. Everything would come in time, Frank told me, and he was right. Rushing things usually just makes a mess.

When you're starting to learn something, it's good to keep at it. When you're just beginning to climb a mountain you need to pay attention to those little steps until you begin to develop some confidence. You just have to have faith that all the small gains you make will add up to something bigger in the future.

But there are also times when what you need to do is take a break. Sometimes your brain gets filled up or your body gets overworked. You'll reach a point where you just can't try any harder. At that point, whether you're learning a new piece on the piano or algebra, it's good to turn your brain off for a while.

Don't worry. You can't really turn it off completely. It'll still be working under the surface, even if you're not aware of it. Your brain can work when you're not paying any attention to it—even while you're sleeping!

But I've also discovered that there are times when my body needs to figure out things on its own, without me or my brain bossing it around. Lots of times I find that it's smarter than my brain. Often you just need to trust your fingers to fly over the piano keys, without thinking too hard. And sometimes it's good just to put that difficult piece of music out of your mind for a while. Come back to it later when you're feeling fresh.

Work hard, but work smart. That's something I've learned from Frank over the course of all the impatient years I've been working with him. If you're smart, you'll listen to your body. You'll take a break and give yourself a rest when it tells you that you need to.

DEALING WITH STRESS

One night when I was about twelve, just before a big competition, my dad heard me talking in my sleep.

Over and over again, I said, "It's nothing, it's nothing . . ." as if I was trying to calm myself down. Hearing that, he worried that I'd crossed that fine line he's always warned me about—the one between discipline and pressure.

The next day he sat me down, and we had a long talk. He told me he loved me and was proud of how hard I was working. But he didn't want me to work so hard that I couldn't enjoy skating. It would break his heart if I wasn't happy.

Some part of me knew I needed to let up. But it took my dad's words to get me to see that I was starting to cross the line. From then on, I continued to work hard, of course. But I tried not to rush myself up the mountain. I tried to be proud of myself for the effort I was making, like my dad was. I tried not to be some kind of lion tamer—demanding more and more of myself, with a whip in one hand.

If you go overboard, you can start putting too much pressure on yourself. It's like when you put a pie in the oven and you can't wait for it to be done. So you turn the oven up too high and it burns up.

If you push yourself too hard, or worry too much about your performance, you can get overcooked, too. That's called stress. Stress is worry, and it's counterproductive. It lowers the ability of both your body and brain to function well.

My parents have always tried to make sure that all my hard work doesn't stress me out. They want me to work hard, but they definitely don't want me to go crazy. One way to check yourself for signs of stress is to see if you can laugh at yourself, even when things aren't going so great.

Here are some more techniques to reduce stress:

★ Relax: lie down and be quiet for 20 or 30 minutes. Take a nap if you need one. Think about pleasant places you've been or seen. Avoid thinking about the things that are causing you to feel worry.

★ Meditate: find a quiet place and, either sitting on the floor or in a chair, or even lying down, try to let your mind become still. Make sure nothing can interrupt you. Take lots of long, deep, even breaths.

★ Play with a pet, or play a silly game (that you don't care about winning) with a friend.

★ Avoid worrying: worry is like a track on your mental CD player that gets stuck and plays over and over. As soon as you realize that's happening, shift your mind onto a different track.

And here are some ways you can reduce stress just before a performance or competition:

★ Play! Sometimes when I'm getting ready backstage before a competition, Frank will make a stuffed animal do the jumps and spins I'm about to do.

★ Relax into your surroundings before a test, game, or a play. Don't get freaked out by all the activity and people. Just look around you and take all of the details in. Try to think of yourself as one more detail that belongs there. You're there because you're supposed to be there. Enjoy the moment.

★ Stay focused: have "tunnel vision" where you concentrate only on the thing you are doing, not outside distractions (who's in the audience, what people will think of you, etc.).

★ Visualize yourself doing your activity well, not making mistakes. (I'll tell you more about this in the next chapter.)

Just remember: feeling your nerves isn't a bad thing. Especially if you're about to perform or take a test, they're a good sign. For one thing, it means you're alive. You're excited and alert. Just watch for signs you may be overdoing it. You want to stay fresh, not stressed.

PROCRASTINATION

Patience has an evil twin, and it's called procrastination. Procrastination is when you put off what you need to do. You know about procrastination: you watch a TV show you don't even care about, instead of reading that book for English class; you play just one more computer game before you practice your flute; you talk on the phone when your room has to be cleaned up.

Do you know what all these have in common? Putting off the inevitable: because you *will* have to read that book or clean that room sooner or later. You're just prolonging the agony.

Everybody procrastinates sometimes, so don't get down on yourself too much. Just think how much better you'll feel after you get your homework done. Then you really can enjoy talking on the phone, instead of dreading what comes next.

It's not that hard to tell the difference between patience and procrastination. Patience is when you're dying to do something, but you know you have to wait for the right time to come. Procrastination is when you really don't want to do something, and you keep thinking up reasons not to. If you're ever in doubt, just ask yourself how you really feel.

TEST YOUR PATIENCE

1) Are you impatient? When you start a new book, do you read the ending first?

2) Do you procrastinate? How many times does your mom or dad have to tell you to do your homework before you actually do it?

3) Are you stressed out? Are there times when you want to scream for no reason?

Everybody's got a little impatience, procrastination, and stress. But keep your eyes open for them so they don't take over your life!

CHAPTER NINE

Imagination

Have you ever noticed how the greatest athletes, like Michael Jordan, make the most ordinary movements—shooting, passing, even dribbling—seem extraordinary? They're extremely disciplined, but at the same time they're amazingly free to imagine new ways of doing things. They manage to turn their skill—whatever it is—into an art. This is true for anything when someone does it extremely well—even math or science.

People think of skating as an artistic sport, and it's obvious why. I skate to music, so I have to be part dancer and part athlete. But skating is no different than basketball: if you want to turn it into an art, you need an imagination that's both disciplined and creative.

Maybe this sounds contradictory. How can you

be creative and disciplined at the same time? Many people believe being creative means throwing away all the rules, while being disciplined requires strictly following them. But that's not really true. The trick is to strike a balance.

PUSH AND PULL

Discipline and imagination are equally important qualities to have. One's no good without the other. But they do kind of push and pull against each other, like a brother and sister who have to live together but don't always get along.

If you're writing a short story for school, for instance, it's important that you follow the rules of grammar. Your sentences need to be clear and make sense to the reader. Spelling and neatness count too. All of that takes discipline and hard work.

But grammar, spelling, and neatness are pretty dry without imagination. To write a story that's original, with surprising twists and turns, there will come a time when you'll need to forget everything else and dig into your own imagination. That's where the answers are, not in a textbook.

Sometimes your imagination will want to break free of the rules. And sometimes the rules will want to tame your imagination. Eventually, by pushing and pulling, you'll find a way to balance them both.

I learned the basic skills of skating by watching others. I listened to my teachers and eventually I learned the techniques I needed. Technique in skating is like the rules of grammar in writing, or the basic skills of dribbling and shooting you need to play basketball. It gives you the tools.

Generally the only way to get the technique down solid is to do things over and over and over again, with concentration. If you've read the same sentence in your history book over three times and still don't know what it means, you're probably not concentrating hard enough.

Maybe that kind of training doesn't sound like much fun. But it is. It takes imagination to picture something new you want to do. Your mind imagines it while your body is learning it, piece by piece. Then suddenly, one day, the two come together and it seems like you've always been able to do it. It's so exciting when you finally figure out how to make your body do a jump or your hand draw a picture the way you've seen it in your mind. Imagination plays a huge part in learning technique.

It works the other way around, too. All of the techniques your body has mastered can also light up your imagination. You might not even know it when it's happening. When athletes reach this state in competition, they call it being "in the zone." To me, it feels like flying. Everything flows together. Your mind and body work in perfect synchrony. You exceed what even *you* thought you could do.

If you watch tapes of my performance as a fourteen-year-old at the Birmingham Worlds, and compare it to my performance at Worlds the next year, or this year, you'll see many differences. A number of those changes were physical and happened in spite of me. Most of all, though, you'll see that at fourteen I was a decent "technical" skater. But I'd only scratched the surface of my imagination. I was far from the skater I am now.

Technique is what you learn by copying others. Art is what you bring to your skating by digging into your imagination—the part of you that's one-of-a-kind and can't be imitated. At fourteen, I was about 90 percent athlete and 10 percent artist. Now what I strive for is 50/50. A perfect balance. And when I find it, I can fly.

DREAMING

I had a huge imagination back then—and still do! But when I was younger, I mostly used it for dreaming. Daydreaming. Nightdreaming. Afternoon dreaming. Don't let anyone tell you it's a waste of time. Even when I was seven and saw myself skating at the Olympics, just like Brian Boitano, I was stretching and strengthening my mind.

Every day since then my imagination has gotten stronger and my dream has become more vivid. Now when I close my eyes, I don't just see myself at the Olympics or on a podium. I see exactly the kind of skater I want to be.

And when I step onto the ice for a competition, I don't feel like I'm about to do a routine. I'm not even thinking about the jumps or the techniques. I've done my hard work. My imagination and concentration are ready. It's too late to teach myself something new now. Falling is the farthest thing from my mind. The crowd fills me with energy. The ice is my dreamland. The music starts and gets right inside of me.

I listen to the music for my program over and over—just listen, without skating. The music and my imagination work on each other, just like my technique and imagination do. And then finally I can see my program, exactly the way I want it to be.

It's like writing a story. If you want to write a good sentence, you have to know what you want to say. Before I can ask my body to do what I want it to do, I have to be able to imagine it in my mind. Remember what I said in the beginning? *If you can see it, you can achieve it.*

★ ★ ★

PUMP UP YOUR MIND

The power of your own mind is very real. If you're into academics, like math, science, or literature, you already know that, since your mind is your main piece of equipment. Without it, you can't do much of anything. But even if your main activity is a physical one, like dancing or rock climbing, only part of your strength is physical. You need to be just as strong mentally to be successful.

Keep in mind another great saying: *You're only as strong as your weakest link.* Imagine a thick chain. If all the links are in perfect shape, it can pull an eighteen-wheel truck. But if only one of those links should break, the chain couldn't pull anything. The same goes for you. Your mind and body are equally important links in your chain, and both need to be strong if you want to be successful.

Backstage before a competition, after Frank and I have gotten settled, I close my eyes and try to see my program, bright and clear, from beginning to end. I take my time and don't rush through it. Sometimes I even see myself falling! And what do I do? Get right up again. Then I rewind the tape and visualize doing it right.

You can use this technique in just about anything you do. Have to give an oral report? Try closing your eyes and seeing yourself in front of the class.

Or maybe you want to get along better with your brother. Maybe the two of you are fighting about something and you're really dreading facing him. You know it will be major fireworks. So, imagine the two of you discussing whatever the issue is, but instead of getting really angry and yelling at him, see yourself staying calm and rational. And if you do start to imagine yourself losing control, see your-self walking away so both of you can cool off. It won't make the confrontation any easier to face, but if you can picture yourself the way you want to be, you'll be better able to be that person when you need to.

Another thing you can do is take the time to daydream. That's right, just sit or lie down and let your mind wander. I don't necessarily mean wish—dream. Just let your mind roam and pay attention to what images and ideas come into it. At the very least, it'll help you be in touch with your imagina-tion. You might also discover some things you never knew were in there.

Try keeping a journal. I do, in little tiny script. Get into the habit of doing it every day. Write what-ever comes into your head—free association. You'll be surprised at what you discover, and it's so much fun to go back and read it later. If you don't want to write, dictate your journal into a tape recorder. Or

STRETCH YOUR IMAGINATION

Here's a way to test and stretch your imagination.

The next time you have an especially interesting dream, write it down. Try to remember lots of details about it.

Now see if you can turn the dream into a short story. Give the characters fictional names. Try to find a beginning, middle and end. Write it up neatly. Check for spelling.

Hand it in for extra credit or give it to a friend to read. See if people don't say, "Where in the world did you get the idea for this!?!"

CHAPTER TEN

Common Sense

O kay, now it's time to stop dreaming for a minute and wake up.

This is the part where I tell you all the things you already know but maybe forgot you knew. I almost shouldn't have to write this chapter, but the fact is that everybody needs to be reminded every now and then to *use their head.*

If you can hang on to your common sense while you're climbing your mountain, you'll be ten steps ahead of everyone else. Everybody's born with common sense, of course. But sometimes people forget where they put it.

DUH

The single most important quality you need to succeed at anything is your health. I don't care whether you're running marathons or playing chess. A healthy body means a healthy mind.

First of all: food. Everybody needs to eat well. Food can be a complicated issue for girls. There's a lot of pressure to be thin. I've figured out that if you're getting a lot of exercise and eating good food, you're as thin as you need to be. Any thinner and you'd be unhealthy.

Say NO to crash diets! If it sounds too good to be true, it probably—make that definitely—is. It's dangerous, too. Please. I mean it. If you really really really feel that you have to lose weight, talk to your parents and your doctor.

Before you decide to diet, observe how you feel. If you feel good about yourself, you're going to look good. If you don't feel good about yourself, it probably isn't just because of how much you weigh.

But if you still insist you're overweight, don't lose weight too quickly. Ask your biology teacher or health teacher about crash diets. They'll tell you that when you lose a lot of fat quickly, you also lose muscle mass, which, believe me, you need. If you don't eat enough, your brain won't perform well. You'll be too cranky and tired to be disciplined, dedicated, or courageous. As you fade away, so will all the qualities you need the most.

Unless your doctor tells you otherwise, a good diet is one that has a lot of variety. Fruits and vegetables, protein and grains, foods with calcium in them. Even chocolate can be all right. Just don't limit your diet to one thing. Mix it up. Don't turn up your nose at vegetables. Instead, see if you can eat at least one of all the different colors of vegetables every day. Okay . . . every couple of days.

(While I'm on the subject of variety, please remember that it's the spice of life. Just as there are many colors and forms in the vegetable world, so is there a great variety of shapes and sizes in the human world. And nature meant for us to enjoy them all. Hooray for variety!)

As long as you're eating a balanced diet, you can always allow yourself a treat now and then. Food is a necessity, but it's also one of life's pleasures. If you never let yourself eat the foods you love, you're suffering *tooooo* much for your dream. If I couldn't have cookies 'n' cream ice cream every so often, you might see a frowning skater out there on the ice. Who'd give a girl like that a gold medal?

SOUND MIND, SOUND BODY

It should go without saying, but unfortunately some kids still don't get it: don't drink or do drugs. They do nothing but mess you up.

Now, a bit on sleep, my favorite subject. Aaaah. I've read that lack of sleep is a big health problem in the U.S. You can't function well if you've had too little sleep. When your body's weak, you get colds and other illnesses more easily. Your face looks bad, too. That's why they call it *beauty* sleep.

Everyone needs a different amount of rest. If you need lots of sleep (like I do) don't be embarrassed about it. If you have to stay up all night just to get your homework done, then you've probably got too much going on in your life. Or maybe you're procrastinating. Try to get your homework done earlier so you can get a good night's sleep.

Get to know your body. Know when it's hungry or tired, and listen to it.

It's also important to ease into whatever you're doing. In sports and other physical activities, stretching is extremely important so your muscles get warmed up before you start working them too hard. Stretching is also vital in preventing injury. But warming up applies to just about any activity. Singers warm up their voices and actors do exercises to get into character. Piano players start their practices by doing their scales, then they tackle Mozart. Even computer programmers warm up by looking at their notes to get their mind involved in the topic before they tackle a more strenuous problem. For me, stretching is a major part of my training schedule.

Another thing to look out for is overtraining. That's when you work so hard at something that you actually hurt yourself rather than help. Most people think this only happens to athletes. But it can happen to anybody who uses any part of her body to do something. Dancers, singers, and musicians all run the risk of hurting the part of them they need to keep healthy, whether it's their toes, voice, or fingers.

If your body is yelling at you, "I hurt!!!" then listen. If you ignore it, it will only yell more loudly. Slow down, and if you have a new pain, get it checked out.

Through most of 1997, I had this pain in my foot. The doctor took an X ray and told me I had a "stress fracture." If I wasn't careful it could develop into a more serious break.

I was worried, but I tried to ignore the pain. I didn't tell anyone how bad it was. So of course it got worse. One day, in a competition, I landed badly on a jump. It felt like someone was stabbing me in the foot, and I fell. Afterward, the doctor told me I should wear a cast and stay off the ice for *six weeks.* This was my Olympic year, the year I'd been waiting for since I was seven years old. At first I couldn't imagine taking a six-week break. Nationals were only two months away.

But finally I used my common sense. I told the doctor to put the cast on. I tried to accept it and relax. I worked on my program in my imagination. And in the end, it turned out okay. I was better in time to go to Nationals, and my performance there was the greatest of my life (to that point, at least!).

You can also apply the idea of overtraining to friendship. If what you want is to be a better friend, keep in mind that there is a difference between being a good friend and being a pushy friend. If you don't give a friend space when she needs it, you could end up ruining a friendship you're trying to strengthen.

So, don't forget: if you use your head, you'll never regret it.

HAVE FUN!

Work hard, be yourself, and have fun! is my motto, and I truly believe that last part is as important as the first two. It's very important to keep up other basic life skills while you're following your dream. Shopping, for instance. Just like you need a well-balanced diet, you need a well-balanced life.

The biggest commonsense advice I can give you is to do things that make you happy. If climbing your mountain is making you miserable, then think about why you're doing it. Probably you started it because

Even at the age of eight, I knew I loved skating.

Eating right gives my brain the energy it needs to perform at its best.

My workouts off the ice are as important as my workouts on the ice.

Because of my busy schedule, I did much of my high school homework on a bus.

No matter how hard Frank and I work, there's always time for laughter.

Picking the right costume is one of the small details most people don't see.

Going from a little girl
to a mature skater was
challenging, but also
a lot of fun.

Makeup was an important part of my transformation.

Lori Nichol, my choreographer, and I work on getting every detail of my routine as perfect as possible.

All those spins take practice, not a gyroscope!

I love the feeling of flowing across the ice.

Having fun with my sister Karen is as important to me as my skating.

Sometimes everything comes together perfectly, like during my performance at Nationals in 1998.

WHERE'S YOUR COMMON SENSE?

Answer True or False to the following questions:

1) My knee is killing me, but I just have to play through the pain. **T/F**

2) It's perfectly fine to lose ten pounds in one week. **T/F**

3) To be really good at anything, you have to do it until you collapse. **T/F**

4) If I were five pounds thinner, I would be a better person. **T/F**

5) If you're having fun doing what you're doing, you're not working hard enough. **T/F**

If you answered False to all of these, then your common sense is right where it should be!

PART II

Getting Serious

INTRODUCTION

Do you want to take your dream to a higher level, maybe even higher than you ever imagined? Well, then it's time to get serious. But first let me clarify that I'm not just talking about winning medals or being the absolute best at something when I use the term "getting serious." One of the most challenging dreams you could ever reach for—being a better sister, daughter, and friend—will never win you an award or bring you fame. You won't stand on a podium while an announcer calls you World Champion Sister. But every time you look in your brother's or sister's, mother's or friend's face, you'll know you've succeeded.

I found out about getting serious when I moved up to Lake Arrowhead to take lessons with Frank at Ice Castle. I'd won some competitions and thought

I knew something about skating. But seeing how hard the really top-level skaters worked and how intense they were about what they did showed me how far I had to go. I'd been skating since I was five, but it was only now, six years later, that I was about to become a truly serious athlete. I needed to really look inside of myself to be sure I wanted to do it.

What made it even more difficult was that I didn't want to sacrifice my relationships with my friends or family now that I was also working to be the best skater I could be. I guess you could say I had two dreams running parallel to each other, and I didn't want to let either one go. Without my family by my side at Nagano, being at the Olympics wouldn't have been so special and my medal wouldn't mean so much to me.

Getting serious at anything requires a whole new level of motivation. You nurture that little spark you had when you first saw your dream. You make it grow into a little fire with discipline, perseverance, and dedication. Then confidence, patience, and imagination fan the flames into a full blaze.

It feels great to reach this point. You've got something special, a talent and dream that are all yours. Remember how big your mountain seemed when you first started looking up toward its peak? Now you've come a long ways up the mountain.

You're nearing the peak.

Some of you still want to go higher. If you do, be ready for some hurdles.

I'm not saying you should get serious. I'm only saying there are some big questions you should ask yourself before you try to do this. Each chapter of Part II poses one of those big questions. I can't tell you the answers: there are no right answers. Each of you can only answer for yourself. But I can tell you how to approach the questions.

By the way, this part of the book is not just for people who want to get serious about a specific activity. The questions, and the qualities you need to find to answer them, will help you as you keep following any dream, even the ones they don't give medals for. And no matter how far you get, you'll always be a champion just for trying.

CHAPTER ELEVEN

Do You Have the Desire?

The first thing you need to be successful at any-thing—at life itself—is motivation and desire. But if you're going to get serious as an artist, scholar, or athlete, and try to reach the top of that mountain, you'll need a whole new level of desire.

Your passion for what you do has to glow even brighter. It really has to burn inside you. You have to feel like you were *made* to be a pianist (or goalie, or chemist, or mountaineer). You can barely contain your enthusiasm for it.

You need to have some talent for it, too. But everyone has talent at something, so it's a matter of making sure you get serious about the thing you really have talent for. Here's the thing: every other person who's serious about the same activity as you will have a lot of talent. Maybe a bit more, maybe a bit less; but in the end it's the other qualities I've talked about in this book that will make the difference. So if your desire to excel isn't burning a hole in your stomach, then I'd think twice about going for it.

THE FACTS

From a distance you might think that my life is just one big dream. I won't lie to you, there are some great things about reaching the level of success that I have. But you'd be amazed at how little time I have to enjoy them. The fact is, to stay at this level takes a huge amount of time and work.

Check out my daily training schedule: I have three 45-minute sessions on the ice, either with Frank or on my own. My gym workouts last an hour, plus I do "on the floor" work (practicing my technique in a gym instead of on the ice). I've added some extra weight-training this year, and I run 3½ miles a day.

And that's just a *normal* day! Then there's the painful yearly ritual of breaking in new skates, and the stress of travel and competitions. There's tons of logistics and business details to figure out—luckily I have my parents and my manager, Shep Goldberg, to handle those for me. I also have to choose my skating costumes, at least three a year.

Just about anything involves equipment and other stuff that you have to take care of. Little details that no one can see, like cleaning your paintbrushes or oiling the gears on your bike, make a big difference. If you advance to the National Spelling Bee, people might mistakenly think spelling comes naturally to you. What they don't see are the hours you spend poring over a dictionary every night. In my case, little details include polishing my skate boots, sharpening the blades, keeping my practice clothes clean, and always knowing where my skating bag is.

You have to be neat and organized, and that extends to your appearance too, even if you're just studying or practicing. All of these are things you have to take responsibility for. If you were messy before, you don't get to be a slob anymore.

SACRIFICE

Oh, and by the way, none of this is free. How much it's going to cost depends, of course, on what kind of activity you take up. At the very least you'll need money for basic equipment, and usually also for lessons or tutoring.

Ice skating can be expensive. Our family didn't have a lot of money when I was growing up, so my sister and I had to make do in all kinds of ways.

Beat-up brown rental skates, then beat-up second-hand skates later. Third-hand clothes, which Karen and I often had to share. Giving up certain toys and things like a stereo so that we could pay for lessons.

My parents had to scrape and save and work double overtime. And I was one of the lucky ones. Lots of skaters have to move away from home to train. But in my case, home came with me!

Now, after many years, I'm lucky enough to be making money at it. But I'll never forget those lean times. Just remember, it's one thing for you to decide you want to devote your life to something. But you can't do it without the support of the people around you. They need to have a bit of that dream too. In fact, it will probably take as much sacrifice from them as from you. You might want to let them read this book when you're done with it!

On a daily practical level, there's the job of getting to and from the place where you practice. You'll either need to develop strong legs for riding your bike, or buy a monthly bus pass, or hope that one of your parents is willing to take on the job of driving you.

Of course, some of the most important things you can do, like be a good sister, don't have any monetary costs attached to them, except for maybe the occasional ice-cream cone. And you won't ever make a lot of money doing them. But they're still worth a pot of gold.

But the biggest sacrifices are personal. The higher the level you try to reach, the less you're able to have a normal life.

I'm close to my family, and close to my friends, but since I got serious about skating I've had much less time to hang out with them. Sometimes I long for a day of just cruising around the mall or going to the beach. I get to do these things, of course, but not nearly as often as I'd like. I went on my first real vacation—ever—when I was sixteen!

THE DRAWBACKS

By now you probably realize that if you do reach a high level of success, it's not all peaches and cream. It's a huge thrill when people recognize you for something you've achieved and tell you how proud they are of you. I'm amazed when someone recognizes me for my skating. But at the same time, it can make you a target, and you have to be careful.

If you have a little bit of success, people will try to use you. If you become popular because of your brilliant performance in the school play, some kids may try to be friends with you because they hope some of your popularity rubs off on them. It's a sad thing. I'm lucky because I have Shep and my parents to help me and protect me. But most people don't have that kind of protection, so it can happen.

Plus, people start to have expectations of you. They create pressure. Sometimes you get taken over by other people's expectations instead of thinking about what's best for you. Either way, you have to deal with them. When you win, everyone loves you. When you fall, you fall alone—with the whole world watching. You can feel their disappointment, and you have to be strong enough to maintain your self-respect through it all.

Even after all the sparkling lights and medals, I still feel like regular old Michelle, and that's how my family treats me. Yet there are so many ways in which you just don't get to be a normal person any more. Anyone who's moved up to higher-level classes in school, or maybe you've even skipped a grade, knows what I'm talking about. In some ways, of course, your world gets bigger and more exciting. But in other ways it gets narrower. For instance, I didn't, ahem, have a boyfriend in high school, and I didn't get to go to a prom.

Being a normal kid might not sound exciting, but believe me it's a big thing to give up. Think hard about it.

This doesn't mean you should give up something you love—it only means you should pursue it for the right reasons. Climbing your mountain because you love it for itself is the right reason. Climbing your mountain because there might be money or fame waiting for you at the top is the wrong reason.

DESIRE'S EVIL TWIN: OBSESSION

Desire has an evil twin. That twin is called obsession. It's one of the risks of getting really serious about your sport or art.

When you get obsessed, you fixate on one thing too much. If this happens, you could miss out on having the perfectly good life you were meant to have. Sometimes it happens to college athletes—they get so hypnotized by the idea of getting into the pros that they neglect their education. Then, if they don't make the pros, they're left behind, and they've got a big hole to climb out of.

I think obsession usually happens when you somehow get focused on the wrong thing. Making a ton of money in the pros is an example. Winning awards is another. You lose the whole picture of yourself as a complete person, and the love that brought you to your dream in the first place.

If you don't check yourself to make sure your desire is focused on what's best for you as a person, then you may end up sacrificing too much. You may miss out on a chance to do something else with those years.

There's no single answer or secret formula for this. You'll just have to know yourself and answer honestly when you ask yourself this question: what do I desire most?

Then all you can do is keep your eyes open and your heart full of love. That's your best defense against obsession and your best chance of having a happy life. Combined with a little luck of course. And I wish you lots of it!

CHAPTER TWELVE

Can You Overcome Setbacks?

I t's easy to have motivation when things are going well. You know how it is—you ace all your finals, the cutest boy in school asks you out, and your hair falls the right way. The real test comes when things go wrong. That's when your motivation will have to prove itself.

Luck plays a part in everybody's life. You always wish for the good kind, but—I hate to say it—somewhere along the line you'll run into the other kind. Even if you've got all the talent and desire and common sense in the world, life doesn't come with any guarantees. You can't take it back and trade it in for a new model. I just hope that your setbacks are small and that there's lots of space between them.

WORKING THROUGH THE BLAHS

The simplest kind of setback is a bad mood. Some

days you just wake up feeling blah, like you want the whole world to go away and leave you alone. There might not be any reason at all for it. You're just having a bad brain day. You might have a whole string of days or even weeks where you're not excited about what you're doing. That'll happen, if you stick with something long enough.

When I was younger, I had my share of bad moods just like everyone else. Sometimes I'd talk about it, sometimes I'd sulk, some times I'd cry it out. Usually Frank or my mom or dad would try to help me get out of it. They'd ask, "What's wrong, Michelle? Can I help?" You should do that too, if you see a friend having a hard day. Just knowing someone can see how you're feeling and that they care makes a big difference.

Now that I'm older, I have my own techniques for dealing with it. If Frank can tell I'm not feeling up to par, he'll ask me what's wrong. I'll say, "Just give me a minute and I'll be all right." I go off by myself and think, or just let my mind relax, or listen to music that cheers me up. I let the feeling pass, and then I'm ready to go again.

For me, sometimes skating itself is the cure for the blues. If you can lose yourself in what you love to do the most, you forget all about your bad mood. If you're a musician, play the pieces you love till you feel better. If you're a tennis player, whack the stuffing out of the ball until you're exhausted.

The main thing to remember is that the blahs will pass. They always do, I've learned. In the meantime, try to get outside of yourself and find your peace of mind. It might be by throwing yourself into your work, talking to a friend or parent or even a pet. Or taking a walk. Or listening to music. By some strange logic, going outside of yourself will help you get back in touch with yourself.

THE TEST OF MOTIVATION

Then there are the bad days (or weeks, or months) when things really do go wrong. One of my toughest months was February 1997, when I fell at the Nationals in Nashville. In fact, the whole winter leading up to that I just felt off. Nashville was the capper. Everyone had said I was unbeatable, and yet there I was, sprawled all over the ice.

It's hard to describe the agony of a moment like that—when you stumble over the most important word in your speech, or blow the last-second layup, or forget your lines in the biggest scene of the play.

It's not just agonizing, but it could be downright embarrassing, *if you let it*. I never feel embarrassed when I make a mistake, and neither should you. You're the one out there, trying your best, not the people watching you. It's natural to make a mistake sometimes. If you never did, you wouldn't be human. Disappointment can be written all over your face, but don't feel embarrassed.

And when you do experience a major disappointment, one that makes you want to crawl in a hole and disappear, this is the time when you need to summon all your confidence, dedication, and imagination to get back on track. The thing that allows you to summon them, the force behind all of them, is motivation. To motivate is to *move*. To come out of your hole and get back into action.

If you're having trouble doing this, think about the word. What's your *motive* for being up on that mountain? Think again about what brought you into it. This is the answer to so many of the problems you'll encounter the further you go: *Get in touch with your dream again*. Remember that everyone suffers failure. Remember why you love your field, separate from your recent setback.

If you can find that, you ought to be able to rediscover your motivation. If you can't, maybe you should reconsider your choice. Maybe you don't want to be in skating, or ballet, or theater after all. If a little bit of disappointment is enough to make you lose your taste for it, then you might want to try something else. Something you'll truly love for its own sake.

PERSONAL SETBACKS

There are plenty of other things that can go wrong. You may wake up with the flu the day you promised to go with your friend to see her favorite band. Or you might have setbacks in your personal life. You might lose a friend who's jealous of the amount of time you give to your discipline, or who doesn't understand your love of it.

When any of these things occur it can make it hard to want to get out of bed. But you'll have to. And you'll have to concentrate on your dream just as much as when you're feeling great. The good thing is that throwing yourself into your work will help you get over the pain faster.

You might also have problems in your family. Maybe a fight with your brother or sister, or with your mom or dad. Or maybe your parents don't understand your dream—not every parent does! It takes some real motivation to keep going through difficult times like that.

I was very lucky because my parents did support my dream. But it still wasn't free. I had to hold up my end of the bargain. Not in terms of winning, but in terms of my dedication. If they ever thought I was just fooling around, they'd say it was time to stop. And if I'd chosen to stop, it would have been fine with them. They didn't push me. The motivation had to come from me, and me alone.

Injury and sickness can be really hard to deal with too. Not only do you hurt, but you can't do the thing you love. Being stuck in bed for a month with mono would be so boring. You would say, "If I have to watch one more soap opera, I'm going to scream!" You have to stay focused on your vision, have patience, and work through the pain and the recovery.

When I had the cast on my foot for the stress fracture, I had to do lots of exercises to keep me strong while my injury was healing. Maybe it was because I had to dig down to find some extra motivation, but when I did compete again, in the 1998 Nationals, I skated my best ever.

Sometimes a setback isn't really a setback at all. But it's impossible to know until you've gotten past it.

BIG SETBACKS

Finally, there are the really, really big things, which I hope won't happen to you: the divorce of your parents, or the illness or death of someone close to you, for instance. For me, it was the death of a dear friend. There's nothing harder in life, unless it's suffering a serious illness of your own.

When a close friend or someone in your family dies, you might be tempted to throw yourself even deeper into your chosen activity. That can comfort you and help you get through the pain. But you shouldn't use it to hide from your emotions: you also need to let yourself feel the grief of the loss.

It was so hard for me to go back to skating after my friend died. Life seemed pointless. I knew he would have wanted me to go on, to keep skating. So that's what I did, and in the end I gained a whole new perspective and appreciation for my life and all the people in it.

But there's another way you might react too. After a tragedy, you might not feel like going back to your dream at all for a while. You should never feel bad if you decide to take a break to deal with your emotions. Your family and friends may need you to be there for them, and that might be exactly the right thing to do.

In fact, you shouldn't feel bad even if you never go back to climbing your mountain. A death or serious illness can change your life. It can give you a totally new perspective on everything. If you truly want to keep climbing your mountain, you'll go back to it eventually. Losing someone close can take some time to heal. And if or when you do go back, I bet you'll have a whole new perspective and appreciation of yourself, too.

CHAPTER THIRTEEN

Will You Do It with a Smile?

It's hard enough to smile through the bad times and to bounce back after setbacks or losses. But for some people, it seems, winning is just as hard.

No matter what you do, you'll have to compete. If you're a violinist, you'll want that first chair. If you're an actress you'll want that plum part. You want to be class president. Wanting to win is a natural urge, and you shouldn't fight it. If your heart's in the right place, then trying to win with all your heart is worthwhile.

But if you're thinking of climbing to the tip-top of that mountain, where there isn't enough room for everybody, then you need to ask yourself how you feel about competition. Do you love it or hate it? Does it make you feel miserable, or does it make you feel *challenged*?

★ ★ ★

RESPECT

If you're lucky, you'll have fierce competition. It'll make you a stronger person and better at whatever you do. Some people thought that because we were always competing against each other, Tara Lipinski and I were arch rivals. But it's not true.

There's nothing better in this world than having a worthy opponent. Serious competition helps you to raise your own standards, keeps you on your toes, and challenges you. If you're competitive in a healthy way, then competition will bring out the best in you.

The healthy quality I'm talking about is called sportsmanship. It means having respect for yourself, your competitors, the officials, your coach, or your teacher. People may say it's missing a lot of the time, but there's still such a thing as respect in life.

It all starts with self-respect. If you don't have that, you'll have a very hard time showing respect for anyone else. If someone is rude to you, you can be sure she suffers from a lack of self-respect. I know how hard other skaters work. I respect them for it, and I hope they respect me, whether I win or not.

LOSING WITH STYLE

One of the best things in life is winning. But it's also extremely important—and good for you, too—to learn how to lose. You have to be generous to the winner, make no excuses, and accept the outcome graciously.

No one can win all the time. Whether it's at play, in a family argument, or in romance, you are going to lose sooner or later. If you look honestly at the reasons for your loss, you'll learn a lot from the experience.

After you've fallen short of your expectations once or twice, you'll be less afraid of losing. You'll understand that it's not life or death. At a time like that, don't be so hard on yourself. If you did your very best, then you have nothing to regret.

SORE WINNERS

If losing makes you mean—to yourself, to your competitors, to your family and friends—you're probably not on that mountain for the right reason. But the same goes for winning. Everyone knows someone who seems to need to win every argument, every game of cards, everything, just for the sake of winning. Is that person you?

If it is, then think again about that original dream of yours. Is it still alive? Still strong? Has it expanded and filled in with all kinds of fun and exciting experiences? Or has the dream narrowed down, become black and white, and zoomed in on one thing:

winning? Has that become your only motivation?

Answer this question with one word: "What do I desire to do more than anything?"

My answer is: To skate. What's yours?

The number-one reason why I've come this far is because, thank goodness, I have such a strong desire to skate. After all these years, I'm absolutely sure that I'm on the right mountain. It looks better and bigger to me all the time.

But let me remind you to look out for desire's evil twin, obsession. With obsession, your world gets too narrow. You tend to forget about important things, like the people around you and their feelings. In a world like that, even winning an Academy Award can seem puny and unsatisfying. There's no graciousness in that kind of world, and no real happiness.

So be sure to look around you. Make sure you're enjoying and appreciating what you're doing. If you're having a hard time being nice to people, and if you can't see the humor in anything, then you probably need to take a break and make sure you're still in love with your dream.

If you are, then graciousness will come naturally. It's a quality that can't be forced. But when it rises up out of you, it's one of the most wonderful feelings in the world.

★ ★ ★

GRACE UNDER FIRE

If you can be gracious, then you have a strong sense of who you are. You don't need to be anyone you're not. You don't need to take anything away from anyone else. You can enjoy other people's success and happiness, as well as your own. You've got your priorities straight. And the only kind of win that's satisfying is one that's fair. One you deserve.

Of course, graciousness comes in handy in bad times as well as good.

People talk about me a lot in the media. Usually they say pretty nice things. But for a year, when I was about sixteen, I heard people talking about my body. Can you imagine? In newspapers and magazines! My body was changing, they said. I took a couple of spills and many reporters said it was because of puberty, because my hips were widening.

I had to go on TV and talk about why I fell at the '97 Nationals. Over and over again, I had to see the video of me crashing to the ice. David Letterman and Jay Leno asked me, "What went wrong?" I just smiled and laughed about it.

I'm not saying it's easy. But part of being a good sport is being gracious to yourself just like you are to your opponents. It's saying, "Well, Michelle, you did your best. I'm proud of you for that."

After a while, it really does seem kind of funny.

My smile on the *Tonight Show* wasn't fake. It was real. Time heals all wounds. Laughing can heal a few wounds too. People who support me and follow my career need to know that my happiness comes from something other than just winning.

CHAPTER FOURTEEN

Do You Love a Challenge?

A competitive person's life is rarely dull, that's for sure. If you want to keep that winning edge sharp, you can't let it get rusty. Anybody at the top of her mountain has to struggle to be patient, like I do. When we see a problem in front of us, we love to turn it into something else: a challenge. Challenge is what excites us. And we don't like to rest until we've met it.

It seems to me that the people who achieve the most are the ones who aren't easily satisfied. Life to them is a never-ending source of new challenges. What about you? When you reach a goal does it make you want to take a vacation? Or, once you've stopped to appreciate your accomplishment, are you ready to move on to the next one?

When you look up at that mountain, does it look too steep? Is the next level about a thousand feet up?

If you're the kind of person who says, "Let me at it!" then you love a challenge. If you say, "I'd rather be somewhere else," then a highly competitive kind of life probably isn't for you. Not today, on this mountain, anyway. There's always tomorrow, don't forget. And lots of mountains to climb.

DON'T FORCE IT

There's nothing wrong with staying home, by the way, or taking on a different challenge, or an easier one. If you find that you're dreading going to rehearsals or lessons or studying, it doesn't mean you don't have talent or courage. It probably only means you need to take a step back. That next challenge will wait for you till you're ready for it. Don't worry. Everybody has to go at her own pace.

Challenge is something that won't benefit you unless you're ready for it. You shouldn't force yourself up that mountain against your will. To be a champion you have to want to keep improving.

Each year it seems I'm working harder than I did the year before. It seems like just when I think I've reached the top, the mountain gets bigger. And, to tell you the truth, I'm always glad when it does. I'd be really really sad if there was nowhere to go but down.

★ ★ ★

PLATEAUS

Occasionally while reaching for your goal, you'll find that you've landed on a plateau—a wide flat area. You're not sure how to keep going. This is a pretty difficult spot to be in. From what I've heard, it happens to everyone. Artists, musicians, mathematicians, athletes, even video-game players.

If you're like me, then you're most happy when you're figuring out ways to get better at what you do. You love to find secret passages up to the next level of achievement. So it can be unbelievably frustrating to be stuck on a plateau.

But there you are. You're as good as you were yesterday, but not getting any better. Working harder doesn't help. Being patient doesn't help. Even your common sense can't help you here. You're without a clue.

That's when you've got to be honest with yourself. Do you still have that spark in your heart? Is your dream still alive? If it is, and you decide to stick it out, then now may be the time to take a break. Read, talk to your friends and your family, listen to music. Let your mind explore other options.

Eventually, you'll have a breakthrough. Things will start moving again, and you'll be back doing what you love.

★ ★ ★

FEAR OF FALLING

In 1997, I had a tough but extremely important year. I've told you a little about it. Now I'll tell you an important thing I learned from it.

The year before had been great for me. I became both the National and World Champions. I was on top of the world. Then the season ended and things quieted down. I looked around and said, *Where else is there to go?* I couldn't see the next challenge. I could only see how far down I could fall.

Instead of reaching higher, I tried to grip my position more tightly. I tried to hold on with all my might. *Just don't fall,* I said to myself. *Work harder. Don't fall.*

Then, of course, I fell. At first I cried and hugged my mom and talked to Karen. Then suddenly I realized—*Wait. That's all? That was the big fall I was afraid of? Have I really lost anything that I truly love? No!* I looked at my medals and thought, *Wow.*

My biggest fears had come true—I had fallen during major competitions. But winning gold medals wasn't the reason I skated. I skated because I loved it. If you're doing something you love, winning isn't why you're doing it, either. So there really isn't anything to be afraid of, because no matter how you placed or what grade you got, you still won, because you tried.

Besides, coming in second or third or fourth doesn't mean you lost. It doesn't matter if it's an audition, competition, or class election, you haven't lost anything. You've done something you should be quite proud of. You've put in the effort, and that, all by itself, makes you a success. Even if you came in dead last, you're still a success if you can say, "I tried my best."

Instead of looking at not coming in first as a tragedy or a catastrophe that can't be overcome, you have to see it as a challenge. That's how I started looking at my falls, and only then did I get excited again. That's when things started happening.

NEW ME'S

Nothing is wrong with reinventing yourself at different stages of your climb up your mountain. Anybody can do it as little or as much as is needed or wanted. I've changed my look—my hair and my costumes—at different stages. Or if the change you're looking for calls for more drastic measures, there are plenty of times during the year when reinventing yourself is not only rather easy to do, it can be downright fun!

After 1997, I started working on a brand-new program. Something completely different from what I'd done before. My programs in '96 and '97 had been dramatic and sophisticated. I had to play a role, like an actress.

In 1998, I wanted to be myself out there on the ice. Lori, my choreographer, made the technique just about as difficult as it could be. But the *feeling* of the music and the movement was natural. It was me.

I wanted to learn how to let the music push everything else—for instance, falling—out of my mind. Instead of only focusing on the details of skating, I opened my mind and expanded my whole *idea* of skating. And it seemed to work. The '98 Nationals were a dream come true for me. I'd taken my skating to a whole new level.

I still had a lot to learn, of course. At the Olympics in Nagano, later that year, my performance was not as electric as at Nationals. But I skated as well as I could, and when I came home with the silver, I wasn't that disappointed. I was proud of how far I'd come in a year, and I knew that there would be more challenges out there for me and more chances to reinvent myself as a skater.

TURNING PROBLEMS INTO CHALLENGES

I see problems as challenges. Being a better skater isn't a problem, it's a challenge. When I find some new way to improve my skating that I hadn't thought of before, I'm always surprised and delighted. Sometimes you just have to go by your gut and follow your imagination, no matter where it leads you, or how crazy it may seem. The worst thing that can happen is you'll make a mistake. So what? Sometimes the only way to learn how to do something right is to do it wrong.

I've always trained hard and thought I couldn't train any harder. But I've still got a long way to go with my skating. There's still a lot more mountain up there—enough, I hope, to take me to the 2002 Olympics and beyond. Skating is only the first of many loves and many challenges in my life. I know there will be many other mountains to climb. So long as there are challenges in front of me, I know I'll make it.

CHAPTER FIFTEEN

Have You Got It in Perspective?

When you're busy climbing a big mountain, it's easy to forget that there's more to life than boulders and cliffs. You can get so caught up in the challenge of the climb that you forget to take in the view. You can't even see beyond your next step. But if you don't stop every now and then to see what the world looks like from up there, then you can't get things in *perspective*.

Perspective is one of the hardest qualities to come by because it requires deep understanding. But it's extremely important. While you're working toward your immediate goals, you need to keep sight of the big picture, or else you'll work your way right into a dead-end. Remember, you've got a whole long life ahead of you.

A VIEW OF THE TRUE

So what does perspective mean? I looked it up, and it comes from the word *view*, or *look*. It means, "The capacity to view things in their true relation or relative importance."

When you're at the top of a skyscraper, you can see the whole landscape below you. You see how all the things down there relate to each other. You can see the true size of things, compared to everything else. Something that might appear big from down on the ground suddenly seems less significant from up here.

Or, try the same experiment on a different scale. Get up really close to a mirror—no, closer, with your face right up to the glass. What do you see? Pores? A pimple? A nose that's too big or too small?

Now step back from the mirror. Look at yourself from a little distance. Now that pimple doesn't seem like such a big deal. Sometimes you need to step away from the mirror in order to see how important—or unimportant—things are in the big picture.

So how does perspective relate to my dream? After Nationals in 1997, my dad asked me a very important question. "So, Michelle," he said, "what did you learn from this experience?" I couldn't answer him at first. I didn't know. So he gave me some hints. He reminded me about perspective.

I thought about the question Dad asked. And then I realized that I'd lost the big picture. I'd forgotten that Michelle the skater is just one part of me, Michelle the person. I'd gotten so serious about skating that I forgot to take my eyes off my skates. It had been ages since I'd worried about anything else. Losing your perspective is not a hard thing to do at all. Say your goal is to someday go to Harvard. You study and study until you think your brain is going to burst. But things are going well. You're getting all A's on your tests. But then, out of the blue, you get a C on a math test. If you start crying because you're sure you've just ruined any chance you ever had at Harvard, then you have definitely lost your perspective. One less-than-stellar grade is not going to make or break you.

Have you ever seen clips of actors and singers before they were famous? Some of those people looked bad and sounded worse. I bet you anything your favorite singer has hit more than just a few bad notes. But she kept the bad notes in perspective and didn't let them ruin her career.

You have to remember that life is so much bigger than getting into Harvard or singing. It includes family, friends, poetry, books, and your whole future stretching out before you.

My parents also reminded me that just because

I'd taken a few spills in competition didn't mean I was a failure. Nobody can be perfect all the time. And anyway, I did end up with the silver medal at Nationals that year. Was that so bad? When I thought about it, I realized that the color of the medal mattered much less to me once I stepped back and got some perspective.

Instead of holding it right up against my nose, I looked at it from a distance and thought about how it fit in with all of my other accomplishments and all the things I still dreamed of doing with my life. Then everything began to make more sense. And I felt that spark again in my heart.

Most importantly, I realized that I still loved skating as much as ever. I get to do the thing I love most in life. How many people can say that? Placing well is important, but the real joy comes from *skating* well.

Ask yourself why you want to go to Harvard in the first place. There are plenty of other great schools all around the world. Is it because Harvard has something special to offer? Or is it just to be able to say you're going to Harvard? If the answer is the latter, than you're working toward your goal for the wrong reason. You should want to go to Harvard because you want the education you can get there, not because of its famous name.

Don't let scores or placements go too much to your head. Losing doesn't mean you're a loser. And winning doesn't make you winner—it just means you did the best within your limits. It's a respectable goal, but not the most important one. I've had days where I've skated below my potential, and yet still won. Those days didn't make me happy. I'd rather skate my heart out and finish lower, if it comes to that.

FINDING PERSPECTIVE

So how can you find perspective? That's a hard question, because when you're buried in all the busy little things of a normal day, it's hard to rise above the commotion. There's only one solution: you've got to set aside some time and make the effort to get some perspective on yourself.

My dad tends to offer me his perspective on perspective all the time, so I can never escape it for very long. Your mom or dad might do the same for you, and I'll bet it's worth listening to them. They might be smarter than you think!

Whether they are or aren't, it's always a good idea to ask someone to give you another view—a view from outside yourself. It might be a coach or a teacher, a friend or a sister or brother. The main thing is, it should be someone you trust to give you an honest view. Then take some time to think about what they tell you. Let their words sink in.

I also think it's good to talk to people in your field who are a little older than you. They'll be able to describe what's in store for you, what's been hard for them, and things you should watch out for. I've learned so much by talking to other skaters like Brian Boitano, Dorothy Hamill, and Peggy Fleming. You never know. After talking to someone who actually goes to Harvard, you might discover it's not the school for you.

In the end, though, you also need to find your own perspective on yourself. Since you can't just observe yourself from afar, I've thought of some more things that might help you rise above the chaos of every day and find a new outlook.

★ Get a view—literally! Take some time (a whole day, if you can) to walk up a hill or in the woods, any place quiet where you can be in touch with the natural world. It will give you all kinds of perspective. Everyone needs to be reminded sometimes that she's a small part of something much larger.

★ Pursue other interests. Reading is a great way to get perspective. It shows you someone else's world. Crafts, hobbies, and games you do just for fun also help give you perspective on the thing you're serious about.

★ Volunteer. There's nothing like helping others to remind you that you're not the only one in the world with problems. In fact, your problems will often times seem pretty puny in comparison.

Now, if you try all of these and find you still can't keep things in perspective . . . then maybe you have a problem. Maybe you shouldn't keep pushing yourself. Maybe you're trying to take on too much. As important as your dream is, you can't let it take over your entire life. You have to be able to grow as a whole person.

After all, you're not climbing your mountain just to get to the top. You're climbing it because you love it. And I hope that right along with that, you're climbing it for a chance to appreciate the view—and how much it reveals about you and the world around you.

Working so hard to get to the top and forgetting to enjoy the view is like baking a cake and then not eating it. So don't forget to stop a minute every once in a while and take a breather. Because it's not only about getting to the top, it's about the fun you have getting there.

CHAPTER SIXTEEN

Sparkle

Y ou may have noticed that *love* runs through this book from beginning to end, like a thread. It connects one quality to the next and holds everything together. A dream with no love is no dream at all.

There are lots of ways you can look at it. Maybe a dream is something that sparks in your heart and then bursts into the flames. Or maybe it's a mountain to climb. Or maybe it's that golden thread I told you about. Remember? I found the beginning of it when I was five and discovered how much fun skating was. Then I followed it and followed it until it showed me that skating was actually my passion.

If it sounds like getting serious requires a lot of sweat and courage . . . it does. But it's all worth it, because at the end of that thread is the greatest feeling in the world. The feeling of accomplishment.

The feeling that you've created something that wasn't there before, and it's yours.

That thread of love will pull you along toward your dream, but it won't do all the work. It can break unless you strengthen it with your own motivation and your own energy. With those qualities, and all the others in this book—and probably a few more I haven't even thought of—your thread can show you the way.

And if you make a dream come true—no matter how big or how small it is—you'll gain the confidence you'll need for the next one.

I've been all over the world, and met lots of people. In certain ways I've led a sheltered life, but skating has given me a pretty good view of what's out there. It's made me very curious about people with different kinds of goals.

Now I'm in college, and I'm making new friends. It was a whole new world for me and I was nervous, but excited as well. It was a whole new mountain to climb. Not that I've given up the old one: I'm not done with skating by a long shot. I want to be in the Olympics in 2002. I'll keep putting in the long hours at the rink. If I don't, how will I ever know how good I can be?

I know how to train for the Olympics in 2002, but how will I fit in on campus? I feel like I'm going to be back in the foothills again, looking straight up, about to embark on another adventure. It'll be the challenge of history and science for me instead of triple lutzes and double axels; books and campus life instead of spins and spirals. But I know what kind of attitude I'll go in with, and I know what qualities it will take to succeed.

I hope this book sparks you to find your passion, and helps you develop the qualities you'll need to nurture that thread. Wherever you feel that spark of fun or happiness, follow it. You won't know where it will lead you till you try.

Eventually you'll find the way to your dream. You'll know it when it's real. You'll see: you'll sparkle, and the whole world around you will seem to be sparkling, too.